T0208387

Into Her World

J. KO

Order this book online at www.trafford.com
or email orders@trafford.com

Most Trafford titles are also available at major online book retailers.

Print information available on the last page.

ISBN: 978-1-4907-6546-4 (sc)
ISBN: 978-1-4907-6547-1 (hc)
ISBN: 978-1-4907-6548-8 (e)

Library of Congress Control Number: 2015915695

Trafford rev. 03/03/2016

www.trafford.com
North America & international
toll-free: 1 888 232 4444 (USA & Canada)
fax: 812 355 4082

Contents

Contents

To Mama Bear and the Bear for all the times y'all have sacrificed for me and still believed in me when I didn't. Thank you for being patient and for letting me reach for the stars. More so when I did not ever want to finish writing or when I struggled in pursuing my dreams. This is only the beginning. Love y'all more than y'all will ever know!

Most importantly, to God for he has given me countless opportunities and talents. I am so blessed and thankful for him being the center of my life.

Foreword

When I was a little girl, my mom and dad both told me I could be anything I wanted when I grew up. They never told me what I had to be or what to study. "Work hard, keep at it, never give up, and you will be successful" was what they always told me. I believed them.

At one point, I wanted to be a marine biologist. Then a zoologist. And after that, an actor.

The only thing my mother made me do was twirl batons. It was a sport and performance to her. We were extremely competitive! From the ages of five to nineteen, I competed on a state, regional, and national level. Instead of summer camps with horseback riding or canoeing, I spent six to eight hours practicing my twirling routines. Like any other teenager, I did not always like the hard work, but I did it anyway because it was all I knew.

Ultimately, though, baton twirling did several things for me that I was not able to acknowledge until later in life. It allowed me to travel as an ambassador to international festivals, compete in the Miss America Organization, and perform at football bowls and professional basketball games. I learned self-discipline and work ethic because I was conditioned to never give up. And most importantly, I learned that I loved performing. Because of my experience performing in front of hundreds of thousands of people, I confidently submitted an audition tape to study at the Western Australian Academy of Performing Arts (WAAPA) and was accepted. During my years of study and working in Australia, I discovered that not only did I love to perform but I also loved organizing work that was to be performed. Producing, directing, writing, acting—simply being involved in theatre or film became what I would do when I grew up. Throughout the past decade, I have had the pleasure of owning a production company, and producing work that employs other actors and artists is more fulfilling than I ever imagined.

I became grateful for the skill and knowledge gained from twirling and enjoyed passing it on to students as a coach. After working with the Australian National Team, heading to the world championships while in Melbourne, I was hooked. I knew that I would always be coaching on some level. I have been fortunate to meet some of the most interesting people through the sport of twirling, and that's how I met J.Ko. I received a phone call after moving to Texas for my husband's work from a young lady who was the featured twirler for Howard Payne University.

Once I met her, I decided that this young lady was one of the most unique, passionate, and inspired people I had ever met. J.Ko is her own person. She looks to no man or woman in today's society for validation. She is motivated by a higher power. That in itself is her validation.

She has also been told that she can be anything she wants to be when she grows up; watching her "grow up" through her college years with that tenacity has been fascinating and awe-inspiring.

In the following pages, you will have a glimpse into her world. From thoughts to prose to words that have simply been laid on her heart to share, she has opened up one of the most vulnerable areas of her world that a person can share—her conscious stream of thought. We wake up in the morning thinking about something. Whether it's something as simple as brushing our teeth or something more intellectual, our minds jump from one subject to the next without our awareness most of the time.

In my line of work, I watch a lot of people. Actors and artists can be some of the most intense people to observe. We are all narrative beings. Forming judgments and opinions happen within a split second for most of us. And whether that judgment and those opinions affect us depends on our perspective in the matter. Are we doing the judging or being judged? Listening to J.Ko experience life as a young lady in her twenties, just trying to do the things she has been called to do, has been an incredibly interesting journey for the both of us. She does not slip into our society's mold of what most young ladies that are twirlers and performers should look like, talk like, or act like. She is her own person. She has found that person by persevering through emotional and physical roadblocks that most have never had to imagine. I have encouraged her through what started as a twirling journey but has evolved into a life journey to never give up and pursue her dreams.

So when she told me that she wanted to write a book, my response was, "Then write, what's stopping you?" The only thing truly stopping her was her. Doubt, self-consciousness, fear—they are only feelings. She channeled those feelings into a productive format and began writing about them on some level.

In a few chapters, you will come across the following words:

There'd never be the time for the realistic points to be addressed
Doubt she'd even be heard
She was only a servant to the land
She wasn't of hierarchy
She didn't fit in with the King's men or ladies
Nor did she aspire to be
She wanted *so* much more

She will have so much more. Because like my mom and dad always said, "You can be anything you want to be when you grow up. You just have to work hard, keep at it, and never give up, and you will be successful." And J.Ko will continue to march to the beat of her own drum and never, ever give up. Enjoy the journey of reading *Into Her World*; may you reach the end of it inspired and ready to be who you are called to be.

Preface

J. Ko was born on May 6, 1988, in the south Texas city of San Antonio. She grew up in the rural town of Karnes City before moving to Stockdale, Texas, which she now calls home. Having the opportunity to be blessed with the ability to see the country and the world because of her faith, education, sport, and music, she has become inspired by the stories she's been told, the people she has met, and her surroundings. For the past ten years, she has been building her collection in the world of poetry and prose.

After a moving conversation with her parents and dealing with a huge heartbreak from a crush, she became more determined to share her beautiful works of words with the world around her. For years, other works have been encouraged and inspired; therefore, now is the perfect time to go public with her unpublished works. Nevertheless, nothing could have predicted the inspirations from each chapter in this book.

This book is only the beginning of J. Ko's talents. She has spent countless hours shifting through her short stories, poetry, prose, and other forms of writing. Those featured in this book are the ones she felt God was giving her the ability to share. Hopefully, every reader can take something away from the book and relate to the inspirational background of every chapter. Lastly, she feels you should never stop believing in your dreams.

Acknowledgments

My family, to my "family" at Texas A & M University–Corpus Christi; Howard Payne University; St. Mary's Catholic Church in Brownwood, Texas, and Stockdale, Texas; my Sigma Alpha Iota and Mary Kay sisters; and my Fellowship of Christian Athletes family members. My baton-twirling coaches and teammates who have given me inspiration and encouragement. A special thank-you—Amber Rhyne Hanel for her tough love, constant belief in me, and being a part of this *amazing* journey, and know y'all each have inspired me to progress in my writings and achieving my dreams. Many of you have helped inspire the stories and poems I have written over the years. Without your willingness to share, I would not have had the ability to write something relatable for others.

Additionally, I have to acknowledge the friends I have met through my travels to Sydney, Australia. Mates, y'all have helped me find my voice and helped me understand who I am as an athlete, artist, Christian, and woman.

Lastly, I want to acknowledge my copy editor, Kristin Bomba, for taking the time out of her schedule to assist in the editing of *Into Her World*. Through her guidance, I was able to present the content to y'all in a more enjoyable manner. Kristin, my gratitude and friendship with you has meant a lot to me. I am thankful for your honesty and tough love throughout the final stages of the book.

Always remember, y'all, don't stop believing and reach for the stars, and you will achieve all your dreams.

Introduction

In life, we experience different events that can lead us to question our own dreams and beliefs and even challenge our hearts and minds. As I have journeyed over a quarter of a century, I have undergone my fair share of ups and downs, heartbreaks, worldly experiences, and being impacted by individuals who changed my life forever. At times, even my faith has been challenged. My heart has been turned frozen to vibrant, and I have learned more about myself than expected. Nonetheless, the impacts of various life events and meetings with the people God sent into my life have allowed me to take a passionate gift and share it with you.

Growing up in a small rural city of less than 1,500 people, about forty minutes south of San Antonio, moving from my father's hometown when I was fourteen because of my education and my sport of baton twirling, I have been witness to a number of ups and downs, which have helped me become the woman and writer I am today. Not having any biological siblings but, instead, being blessed with a godbrother, two godsisters, and six feline siblings, I had much time to occupy and was able to use my individual time to write out my thoughts and emotions. Never in a million years did I ever dream about sharing my writing with others.

My travels with the sport of baton twirling, education, and for family have allowed me to visit several states; the island of Maui, Hawaii; and twice, the country of Australia, where I cannot wait to go back again. Constantly, I am reminded of the little things that inspired me throughout each journey I have taken. Never once did I forget to go after my dreams or give up. For I believe nothing is impossible with the help of God, and he has great plans for us to prosper.

After years of writing and receiving encouragement from people around me, I decided it was time to share my works that remained in a blog, spiral, or hidden diary. The hardest part was selecting which pieces should be shared with you. Many times, while working on my undergraduate degree at the one and only Island University, Texas A & M University–Corpus Christi, and at the pride of the Pecan Bayou, Howard Payne University, for my master's degree in youth ministry, I found myself working on poetry and prose when I should have been researching, studying, or writing papers. I can even remember the nights working at a parts store in Brownwood; it was so dead in the store I'd just find scratch paper and write. Ultimately, this small-town Texas twirler girl's writing has been a book in the making for over ten years.

Throughout this book, you will discover I have written poems, songs, short stories, and letters based off of the chaos and craziness God has thrown at me. Through weathering the various storms, I have discovered I may not be the only person traveling through the same storms. Ultimately, we can take the lessons we learn from our own personal experiences and help others in their time of need.

Within each poem, story, and letter, there is a story of inspiration worthy of being shared. After eight years, two universities, and two degrees, I feel now is the appropriate time to share my most private thoughts and writings. Often we are told there is no time like the present and we have to take one day at a time. Now is the time.

While you go through the various stories, sit back, enjoy, and feel free to read them over and over again. The stories have been placed in different categories to help you understand the way my mind thinks and for you to target stories you might need to help you right away. Most importantly, this is an opportunity to learn from someone's past, emotions, and feelings. I only ask that you keep an open mind and soul.

Several years ago, my own mother told me I had been given the gifts of writing and creativity. I really did not want to believe her because I had never made the poetry and prose team in middle school or high school, although I did make the debate team all four years of high school. No matter where I was, I always found myself taking out a pencil and paper to write down my thoughts. The inspiration I received came from my experiences, emotions, surroundings, and so much more. It was not until just recently that I learned my works should be shared.

Although I was shy when the idea was first presented, I owe a huge thank-you to a former University of Notre Dame, Sydney, Australia, coworker. This coworker loved reading the blogs, songs, and poetry I would share with her. I often joked I would love for her to sing one of my songs with her band one day. Nonetheless, some of her last words of encouragement were "You have a gift. Don't let it go to waste. Never be afraid to share your words with others."

Since the time I spent in Sydney, I have become even more encouraged to share my works. The only problem has been choosing the ones I have felt appropriate to share with you. Keep in mind—the words I have written have come from God, not me. Without him, I could never have had the ability to write or the courage to share my experiences with you. Remember, to write is to ignite the soul and never be able to share what is in your heart with others.

Chapter 1

About a Boy

One guy can make you hate all the guys and everything about them, but one man can walk into your life and love you for who you are and show you that not all guys are the same.

—London Monds

Each poem and prose piece in this chapter has been inspired by a boy or two who has been able to touch my heart. As London Mond said, "It is possible with one glance for a boy to touch a girl's heart, one to break her heart, and one to put her heart back together." Each boy being described has played a vital role in the shaping of my thoughts, my feelings toward the male race, and the woman I have become today. Nonetheless, the inspiration from each of the three boys—the hunter, the punter, and the hoopster—has changed me for the better.

The Hoopster

A man I once knew, who taught me how to pay it forward, treat others with kind respect, and never judge a book by the cover. The hoopster was someone who inspired me as an athlete and a person, changing my life. Although our time together as friends was very brief, I know he will forever be in my heart.

Dark-Eyed Stranger

She sees him from a distance
Majority of the time
He's sitting all alone
Spiritually he's not alone
Whenever she notices him
She thinks privately,
There sits a godly man
With a pure heart and soul only
Distilled with the heavenly Father
Not to mention a great physique.
Each time she sees him
He's always smiling and full of life
Something not always common nowadays
A part of her always
Wants to carry on a friendly chat with him
But she's completely timid for several reasons
She longs to befriend him and know his story
However, she cannot
Her soul is truly torn in half
She's full of resistance and fear
She's afraid with just one look
Into his bold, daring, mysterious dark eyes
She'll simply fall
Fall so fast and completely unravel
Not knowing if she'll be caught
Yes, she does believe
This pure, wholly godly man
Could catch her before she crashes
But another part of her believes
It'll be just like always
Her intentions misread
And her Southern kindness misunderstood
She'll end up falling flat on her back

No one there to catch her
And she'll be scarred, bruised, and broken again
On to see the deer running back into the woods
Where he came out of
Nonetheless, from far off in the distance
She only prays her heavenly Father
Will continue to let the dark-eyed stranger
To do his will
From a distance
She vaguely prays for the dark-eyed stranger

Lord, I Often Wonder

Sometimes I often wonder, Lord
How we can be caught up in our
Own business of our lives
Yet we are unable to truly see
What has been in our presence

For such a long time
It is something that resonated
In the back of the mind
However, never acted on

Often I wondered how he would just sit alone
I know a part of me believed he was in his own world
Not really hiding behind technology
Never a reason to invade a man's privacy
Still, a part of me wondered if there was more to the story

As time passed us by
And the world came to know him
Really, before that
I could sense nothing but goodness and righteousness
I could tell this man was a man of God
What caught my attention the most
He wasn't like anyone I'd met before

Even as the world got to know him more
Even at my personal weakest moment
Not when I needed was Superman or a knight
God, you somehow pushed him to rescue me
So I embraced his warmth and grace
That you provided him with
Somehow this moment only reassured me
That my heart and intuition were right

How could I have been so blind
How could it take a tragedy for me
To see that you send angels into our lives
To help make it through various moments
And the gift of friendship is such a blessing

All I know is
I wanted to ask your human son
What he sees in his reflection
Maybe in time I'll be able to express
The words I'm meant to tell
I believe I am meant to speak the truth and your word
Yet I still believe
You've blessed me with the ability
To understand in a way
What he's been going through

Granted, our time may be cut short together
Lord, I just ask for your help
I am no longer a fool
Help me to show care and appreciation
Let me return the favor
I know you have great plans for all of us

The Punter

We all meet that one boy who captivates us and turns our worlds upside down. He is the one who rocks your world and leaves you completely starstruck. In a part of your mind, he is the perfect boy for you, or at least the one you dream about. He has the charisma you can never forget. Yet when you find yourself lost and falling in too deep, all your walls and morals start crumbling. Nonetheless, his voice, eyes, face, and personality are tattooed on your mind. In the end, you are the idiot.

When You Look into the Mirror

She gazes from afar
Only to notice a man
Surrounding himself with books and technology
Many times her curiosity
Would cause her to wonder,
Was he using it all as a shield?

As days turned into weeks,
Weeks turned into months,
Her curiosity grew
As the same patterns repeated

There he would be
Sitting alone, and shouldn't have been
A part of her wanted to ask him,
"What do you see when you look in the mirror?
Because if you saw what I saw,
You would *not* be hiding
You would not be the lone wolf"

Sometimes she longed to tell him
What she saw when she looked at him
For the longest time, she could see this
A man who was very Christ-like
Although not perfect, yet honest, humble, and loyal
Something that many men are

This man has class and chivalry
He's very kind, caring, soft-spoken, and gentle
Not to mention has a really huge heart
A heart distilled with hope, faith, and love
He sends off a vibe full of positivity and safety

He is a great friend, and she's almost certain
His family is extremely proud of him

Call her crazy for wanting to be honest, but to her
This man was awesome and amazing
It's not every day you meet a man
Who does something without asking

Or, after you've just cried your eyes out
Despite not wanting to be comforted,
Allows you to collapse in his arms
He is everything that God
Knows you really need
Who could have asked for a better person in your life?

Oh, how blinded she could be
Unable to truly see how much
She values and appreciates this man
Nonetheless, she only prayed
For his true happiness and for the best

It's amazing how God works
How his love can be shared
And be given to others

To her this man's presence
Has only made her want to be a better person
To continue keeping a strong bond with Christ,
And to continue staying on the right path
And how the little things make a difference

Maybe one day
This man will be able to see
How she sees him
And understand things
Mostly how he's been able to make
An impact on another's life

Wanting to Escape to Neverland

It seemed he rode into town
On his steel-ton horse
Appearing to the crowds
Expecting to be cheered on
By all that were gathered across the land

As he came into town
Everyone made way for him
Regardless if he appeared
To be absorbing the limelight
Treating people one way in public
Yet privately mocking them
Showing no signs of gratitude
Just letting arrogance get in the way

She couldn't bear to be a witness to this
She wanted to stand up to him
Yelling at him his ways
Truly needed to change
And he needed to take a look in the mirror

What happened to the man
Whom she was honored to know
Excited to be associated with
Live in the same land with
The man whom she defended
Without a blink
Just trusting her faith

Now she just sees
A man who is riding on a steel horse
Who is secretly letting his pincers come out
A man who knows how to show

His cold, ruthless, and emotionless side
A man who appears to have nothing but a stone-cold heart

She knew he once was wrapped in caution tape
He had a big flashing warning sign
She had been warned the man wasn't what he appeared
He may have appeared to be a man of worth and service
But deep down she knew the truth

Somehow, on her path to self discovery
She was able to see past the mask he once wore
And see that he was just a man
Wearing a people-pleaser mask
That underneath it all
He was nothing but
A man who was lost in his own world
A man who could appear to be someone
The world would be proud to know
Call a hero

Still, somehow that man had disappeared
Over the past months of knowing him and observing him
She felt that man she once cared about
Had just been an act
And should have known he was trouble from the start
She wished she could go back and change things
But damage had already been done

She just wanted to fly off to Neverland
A land where he had no domain
Where he couldn't play people for fools
Nor read too much into their gestures
Assuming something was more
Than what it really was deep down

No, Neverland would be the place
Where people were free of judgment
Treated equally no matter what

There was no ruler but God
No one to tell people what they should feel or think
No one to question their emotions or others

The first moment she could escape
The same land as this so-called man
She would take a one-way ticket to Neverland
She wouldn't have to fear the man and his entourage
No more ungratefulness occurring
No more having to see
Others not having confidence
Or filled with insecurities

So until then,
She would just pray he'd get a reality check
He'd come to his senses
Grow up a little
And maybe,
Just maybe, see there were people who cared about him
For the man he could be and once was
Yet this all seemed highly doubtful

Eventually, though
She escaped the King
And freely soared in Neverland
Forgetting that he had ever existed
Or waltzed into her life

Guarding Her Heart from the King

She guards her heart
Refusing to let the King and his court
See the truest colors of her golden heart
She tried her hardest to express her kindness and gratitude
Serving them with a polite smile, respect, and friendship
Never once really shouting her innermost thoughts
Most certainly never wanting to disrupt the peace

Even when she didn't always agree with the King's decisions
She only showed her greatest sincerity towards him
Respecting him and supporting
Or at least tried to show him she supported him
Throughout his trials and tribulations
Yet deep down
She could see beyond his crystal sapphires
That shielded his soul from the rest of the world

Regardless if he refused to demonstrate
His softer, gentler side to the world
She knew that man existed
However, she knew the King
Wouldn't let the world or his men see
Most likely the land wouldn't understand it
Nevertheless, who was she

She was just a mere servant to the land
Reporting the news
Entertaining the crowd like a jester
A scholar in training
Who observed the people in the land
With an open mind and heart
Seeing things differently from others
So she's been told

Refusing to get caught up in the King's web
Acting like the norm
Continuing to live her life and holding her own

Oh, but deep down
She did hold her secrets that
Would take a wise man to unlock
She may not wear her heart on her sleeve
Nor express the feelings of the heart
She was enjoying not being in the spotlight

For she did not truly despise the King at all
There was something more
She knew what she wanted to tell the King
Yes, a private matter of the heart
Still, it wouldn't be something she'd share openly
The only way she'd share it
Would be on precise terms
Maybe when all the fall leaves abandoned their trees
Or when the rain ended the drought
And met half her age in combined attacks
She'd unlock the mystery to the King
Nevertheless, she knew the truth of it all

When would the King realize
She could see beyond his front
And not go anywhere because she understood
It would come to surface again
To confront him about it
With the busy lives of the land
There'd never be the time for the realistic points
To be addressed
Doubt she'd even be heard

She was only a servant to the land
She wasn't part of the hierarchy
She didn't fit in with the King's men or ladies
Nor did she aspire to

She wanted *so* much more
To fit in with the Heavenly King
She wasn't someone groveling at his feet
Begging to serve him at the drop of a hat
She was someone who did speak her mind to him
Still, she had her reservations

Beyond reality
She knew she had to guard her heart
Hide her emotions and feelings
Stand firm in her convictions and morals
Continuing to live, work, train, and serve
Never changing to please another
Staying focused on her ambitions
As she had been doing
Before she even knew the King

All she knew was
She had to be careful
And not get her hopes up
Only pray the King
Could one day see
He was more than what
He appeared to the world to be
He was a man of faith and worth
Most importantly
He too, had a servant's heart of gold
He just had to remove his crown

But that day
Will be the day
When he sees
That every mystery
Is full of beauty, grace, love
And has the ability to be solved

One More Hour to Go

There was the road she was driving on
She knew where she was going
She had driven this path for the past four months
Yet today's drive seemed a little different

She couldn't seem to wrap her head around a few things
No way in a million years would she have believed
She'd be back in competition mode
Working on fulfilling her dream
Overcoming the odds
Doing what people wouldn't have expected her to do
Still, a part of her felt shattered

About a month after her training
The unexpected occurred
She never expected to have her path
Cross with the King
And to start to see the compassionate, caring, gentler side
A part of her had actually missed this King

But as days drifted away
Summer turned to fall
She soon realized that she had gotten in too deep
She had believed in her heart
That the King was a good-hearted man
Not a ruthless boy full of arrogance
He had changed from the ways others in the land
Had been describing him, viewing him, and judging him
She chose not to listen
Only defend him to others

People called her blind, foolish, and other names
Saying she wasn't in her right mind

These words burned her soul
They came from people who supported her throughout her journey
She only wanted the world to see what she did
Once the boy king took off his mask
And stopped hiding away from the rest of the world

For some reason
She began to trust him
Against her own way of being
She never let her guard down, put her trust in anyone, or opened up
What was she doing
How could this be happening to her
How could she
A servant of the land
Respect, care, admire, and want to befriend a King
Who in return
Now only showed his vindictive, cruel, and cunning ways

Somewhere along the way
The man she wanted to know
The man she thought cared for her
As a human being
Forgetting she was only a servant to the land
Had disappeared
And become the King the land believed he was

She'd had enough
A part of her wanted to walk away from him
A part of her still believed that somewhere deep down
Was the man of worth, faith, kindness, and everything
She felt, saw, and got to know
When their paths crossed
On that dreary summer night
He was better than the boy he presented himself to be

As time grew near for her
To enter the world of competition
She missed the King

Whom she thought was someone
Who understood her and could relate
She missed their conversations, jokes, and exchanges of smiles
However, she knew it was all over now
The King chose his crown and his hierarchy of people
The "beautiful" and the "rich"

Although her heart would be torn by confusion
And she might never be able to understand
The meaning behind the King's mood swings
She'd never forget the way he did show his heart
At one point
But at that time
She had to say she was done
She'd worked too hard
To worry about someone
Who apparently
Only cared about himself and not the representation of his character
She was done making excuses

While she continued to shift her mind back to the road
She knew God was in complete control
And knew exactly what was going on
Maybe one day the King would become the man
She knew he could be
Not the boy he turned out to be
She only had to walk by her faith
Not by her sight
And never stop believing
Or underestimating perfection

She looked at the clock . . .
One more hour

The Hunter

Everywhere you go, there are possibilities of meeting someone who has a completely opposite personality from yours. At first you see the person from only their outer shell, but when the time is right, you realize the heart of the person. Do not let me fool you; the Hunter and I did not always get along. It really took God's hand to create an interesting friendship.

Prayer for a Golden Greek

I look at you and all I can do
Is pray for you and your soul
Everyone believes you're the Golden Boy
Who has been blessed with talents
And sent here to distill the nation with hope
Your stride suggests
You've been given great pride
Which you're unafraid to hide
You've got the whole world
Eating out of the palm of your hand
They all believe you're their hero
Defender of the night
However, I see something completely different
I look at you and see the truth
On the outside
You seem as if you're a part of the populace
And you're a Greek god
Simply blessed with abilities from the heavens
Able to treat the world the way
Your heart desires
But deep down I can sense
You hate acting the way
The populous encourages you to be
Though in public you treat others a certain way
When you turn them around or speak privately with them
When no one is watching
You'll let the good ol' boy out
Admitting your faults
Being a respectable gentleman
With a humbled heart and gentle spirit
Someone the world
Should truly admire
Not the untouchable Golden Boy

You claim to really be
The person that secretly
Many of your peers speak ill of
And do not understand your estranged actions
Secretly I know, I wish and pray
You'd always allow
The admirable, respectable, and humble side to show
Not ignoring people
Who are not a part of the populous crowd
Just being someone all the men want to be
And all the ladies adore
And shower you with
The sweet and loving affection a god deserves
But who am I to suggest anything
I am just a bystander
Who has been subjected to your actions

Observing things from a corner of the world
Caught in your unhealthy crossfire
All I can say to you is
Although you can be a great golden god
I see into your eyes and believe you are hiding
You are the only one who can analyze your actions
Change your ways for the better
Just know this
Our Heavenly Father is watching
Not everyone believes you're the Golden Boy
The untouchable Greek god
Until you can be the real and truthful you
You'll never really be true to yourself
And receive the greatest gifts and blessings
Until then, I'll pray for you!

Chapter 2

Honor and Inspiration

No person was ever honored for what he received.
Honor has been the reward for what he gave.
—Calvin Coolidge

Miller and Hollywood

Over the years, I have had the opportunity to meet some of the most amazing people. Part of my inspiration are the school and students I worked with my last year as an undergraduate, who made me see life from a completely different perspective. The other part of my inspiration came from a man I got to know my first year of graduate school. This man inspired me and encouraged me and really was like a big brother to me. Those students and Hollywood will live in my heart forever.

What Makes a Buc?
For the Roy Miller Buccaneers

What makes a Buc?
Is it the value of education he receives,
The gifts and talents he has,
The athleticism he has,
Or even something more beneficial?
No.

The heart of a Buc
Is so pure, alive, and strong.
Bleeding purple and gold,
Beating out a song
That always keeps the body going,
Never afraid to take a leap!

The mind of a Buc is full of balance and brilliance,
Always open and ready for success.
A mind charged with knowledge and inspiration
By the most amazing, gifted, and inspirational
Leaders and teachers of Roy Miller,
Never giving up on their Bucs,
Assisting them as they "shoot for the moon,"
Encouraging their minds to grow and letting them take a shot.

The body and soul of a Buc is
Infused with positivity from his heart and mind,
Constantly striving to be extremely powerful,
Full of strength,
Inducing the body and soul
With so much hope, inspiration, and motivation.
Thus, these components provide
A Buc with the possibilities
Of stepping out onto the field with his brothers,

Ready to throw that pass,
Defend his blind side,
Never letting his opponent pass by him.

A Buc is a unique champion
Provided with so much more than tangible objects,
Given guiding stars to help him leave
His footprints in the sand.
Knowing that regardless of anything
He can achieve greatness and become his own star.

For a Buc
It is all about his heart, desires, and dreams.
Never giving up on himself or his brothers,
Being more than just a team player,
Always bleeding purple and gold,
And remembering from the moment he dons
The purple-and-gold uniform,
It's more than just an ordinary uniform—
It's what makes him a Miller Buc!

Purple and Gold

Purple and gold
The colors they bleed
With all of their hearts
The colors of the walls
Embraced with magic
As they walk through the halls
Of Roy Miller
From the first moment
They become a "Battlin' Buc"
To their very last days
Of waltzing the halls
That their hearts bleed
They will always be a Buc
And will never walk alone
Because their hearts bleed
Purple and Gold
And have been touched
By people who believe in them
Instilling each and every Buc
With love, hope, and inspiration
Always encouraging each Buc
To continue bleeding the colors of
Roy Miller High School
As they reach for the stars
Achieving their aspirations and dreams
Constantly remembering the magic
They first felt
When they embraced the walls
Of the magical Miller halls

Hooray for Hollywood

In memory of Chris "Hollywood" Jones.
Published with permission by Chris Jones's family.

Hooray for Hollywood
Your music lives on with us forever
Your beat will always be heard
And your experimenting and compounding will always be seen in the lab

Your star may never land on the Hollywood Walk of Fame
But it will always be on the HPU Walk of Fame
You left a legacy
One that will never be forgotten
You didn't know a stranger
You were always joyful and full of life
You were never afraid
Always ready with a big ol' bear hug

Regardless of where you are
Your star will *always* shine bright
We'll constantly need to wear shades
You'd probably think that's cool

Now that you're riding with angels above
You'll always be remembered
As the James Dean of our era
Leaving a star to shine brighter and brighter
Dreaming as we're going to live forever
And being remembered as a great man, brother, and father
Called before his time

So here's to the good times
The smell of chocolate after marching on Old Main
Taco Bell and Taco Bueno
And singin' "Little Liza Jane"
Hooray for Hollywood!

Chapter 3

Merry Christmas and Happy New Year's

It is the personal thoughtfulness, the warm human awareness, the reaching out of the self to one's fellow man that makes giving worthy of the Christmas spirit

—Isabel Currier

Merry Christmas and Happy New Year's!

Every year at Christmas, it seems I am always wishing for something very special and personal. One year, I decided I should write out my Christmas wish. Coincidentally, it seemed to carry into the New Year. As the song "Please Come Home for Christmas" says, "If not by Christmas, by New Year's night."

New Year's Wish

It's January first
Where were you at the stroke of midnight
When everyone was wishing "Happy New Year"
Were you with the ones you love
Were you opening up
That bottle of bubbly
Did you make a toast
Did you make that New Year's wish
Have you written New Year's resolutions
Mostly what I'm curious to know
Is did you get to kiss your sweetheart
When the New Year began
Did you make that wish
That you too could be
With the soul you long to be with
That one whom you believe all your dreams
Can be shared with
Or did you do something crazy
Like go outside
Look at the beautiful New Year's stars
And find the brightest one
To find yourself
Wishing upon it
A part of me wonders
Did you make a wish
That you and I could have brought in
The New Year together
Or did you even make a wish
For you and me

Chapter 4

Facts of Life

Life is what happens to you while you're busy making other plans.

—John Lennon

Life

The poems presented in this section are illustrations of how our surroundings can affect us. Also, how busy the world around us can be as life happens. We all have been through so much, which all of us can relate to!

For Good

As the hours count down and the minutes pass by
One can only imagine the anticipation that is swirling
Around in one's very own stomach
It seems so impossible
That three years have come and gone
It doesn't even feel like
The time has come and gone
It seems like just yesterday
I was beginning my journey
With the shoe on the other foot
Embracing my gift of music and helping our future
Often, I believe none of this makes any sense
Yet I know
As things come to an end
You have to think back on the amazing memories created
All I know is that deep down,
I have been transformed
And it's all because of those
Who have accepted me
Allowed me into their lives
And been the best campers a girl could have
Through the small family
That has been created
The connection is eternal
We all have been transformed
For good

I'd Go through This Again

I may have called the day
Getting all dolled up
Thanks to someone blessed
With beautification talents
To pay a visit to the dark-eyed stranger
Stupid, a waste of time, ridiculous
Yet in my heart
I wouldn't have changed anything

I knew it was God's plan
And I'd like to thank the woman
Who helped me get out of
My typical comfort zone
For once I actually let someone
Take control, pick my wardrobe
Make me glamorous

I had no objection deep down
On the outside
I was freaking out
This was all new to me
I'd never done this before
Nor had I really cared

If you ask me
I'd go through this again in a heartbeat
To allow someone to help me enhance God's beauty
To feel a little extra
On top of the world
Letting a hidden side of me shine
To feel like a shining star
All thanks to the kindness of a friend

Revelation of a Secret

We all have our secrets we don't boast about to the world
Sometimes we want to keep them hidden
Not that we're ashamed of what they are
We just want to be humbled and a servant
We want the spotlight off of us
And the attention on those who truly deserve it

Often we feel that the secrets
Should just be confided to those
Who really need to know
Not to worry the rest of the world about things
Not because of shame, more so about privacy
Yet these secrets can be a mystery to us as well

When we least expect
The revelation of the secret
Begins to surface
And you have to be truthful
Sometimes the truth may be hard to face
Other times the truth is perfectly natural
Completely honest and spoken with the words God's provided
Although one might wonder what the world would think
We can't allow fear when the truth
Does become a part of reality

Sometimes it is difficult
To tell someone you want a normal life
To be treated like the rest of the people who walk the planet
To not let titles, honors, or accomplishments define you
To just go about the day-to-day
Not letting the other side affect you

Just remember, God is your quarterback, your captain, and commander
He has everything planned out for us all
Even when we're disclosing a part of us
If it does become public
Never be afraid
Or never be afraid
If the time is right to tell your story
And get your secret off your chest

All I say to you, world
Just tell me what you want to know
And when the time is right
I will reveal all to you

Most importantly
When you least likely expect it
The truth does reveal itself
And you have to let God guide you

Here's to the List

She started thinking the other night
As she wrote her best friend
Some two thousand miles away in a jail cell
Telling him about her twenty-fourth birthday
Midway through the letter she started reminiscing
Joking with him about the time when they first met
And when he called her out from the start
Yet as the years progressed
She eventually created this image
An image of a man she knew would *never* exist
However, by the end of this section of the letter
She was able to tell him that he was right all along
A part of her knew in her heart
She'd never settle
For a man less than the one
God had prepared for her and created in his likeness
Even though jokingly she knew
He wouldn't be riding in on a white horse
He would be driving in
In a beat-up ol' white car or truck
Born and raised in the country
Maybe labeled a redneck or cowboy
A redneck or a cowboy who praised God
And believed in God with all of his heart
Understanding that God and he had an unbreakable bond
It's funny, though
She kept on telling him that the list
It wasn't worth keeping
So she decided that she'd place it
Somewhere no one would see it
For that time, she thought of perfection
Where'd perfection take her?
Perfection took her to a place of

Unhappiness and endless hopes
Somehow she forgot who she was
She even admitted to her friend
She didn't want to write him or communicate with him
However, God chose to step in at the right time
Was it blowing out all twenty-four candles on her cookie-cake
Or was it praying so hard she'd find answers?
Nevertheless, she told him when she started packing
She found her list again
And in finding that list
Her smile and laughter returned
Faith does some tricky things
If only he could talk some sense into her
But what did it matter?
All she knew was that
This was her schoolgirl list she had created
A list she had created on her thirteenth birthday!
One day she knew
The man reading this letter would be laughing at her
Her adoptive sister would be saying, "I told you so"
And her Church family would be saying, "St. Stan, thank you!"
But for now, she had to own up to it
In her heart, she'd always been praying
To see that beat up ol' white car or truck
Driving up that dusty road
Out would come her dark-eyed
Redneck
God-loving
Cowboy
Ready to take her away into the Texas sunset
To lie in a sea of bluebonnets at night
Underneath those bright Texas stars
And by sunrise
They'd realize that God's love was at work
Joining these two souls
So here's to the list.

My Life Could Be a Country Song

My life could be a country song
Full of heartache and sorrow
Yet full of life and overcoming the odds
Sometimes I wondering what it'd be like
To write a song about my life
Talking about every moment
Living it and embracing it
Constantly I find myself
Thinking about the little things
And how they can make such a difference
Maybe even if we live in different worlds

They say it's time, girl
For you to just be patient and hold on
Silence your thoughts and words
Don't lash out, even if the world's wrong
And only listen to what God tells you
Maybe when you stop trying to
Save the world and run from your own fears
You won't be so blinded and you'll see again
And know where you're headed

Having faith isn't always easy
But it's something we must have
Even when we want to yell or scream

Piled behind It All

There she sat
Seeing her reflection in the rearview mirror
Seeing a girl who has spent the past eight years
Growing in her faith
Pulled into stacks of books
Staring at a computer screen
Spending countless hours researching
Training until her body ached
Traveling the globe a time or two
Experiencing things she'll cherish forever
And learning from the not-so-great experiences
Yet at the end of the day
There was a hole in her heart
And a pit in her stomach
She pondered what was missing from the equation
Was this all she was meant to know?
She was a big dreamer
From a small Texas town
Who wanted nothing more than to succeed
And to have all her wishes come true

Silence emerged in the car
She felt there was a barricade around her heart
Deep down she was afraid to admit
She was just like any other woman
She longed for God to develop her faith and heart
Fully prepared to accept
All he would give her
She always prayed God would answer one prayer
Nightly, she prayed for the one
The one he created just for her
The one with whom she could fulfill the
Call to the vocation of marriage and family

Constantly serving him and his people
Raising their children to be ambitious servants
Who would learn the beauty of all His gifts
The price His Son paid for us
The value of faith, hope, love, and virtues
The meaning of serving and loving Him
'Til it hurts
The one with whom she could see the world
Take crazy adventures
And create priceless memories
The one he chose
To bring out the best in her
And help her become a better
Bride of Christ
He would be the one
To push her, challenge her
Support and encourage her
And the one whom she could
Return all the endless love he gives her

She sighed
She'd made lists of perfection
Tried to find fault in herself
And her inexperienced self
As reasoning to push people away
She was one hot mess
Who would ever believe her
About her wildest desire
She was always in a hurry
Soaking up knowledge
Serving others
Falling more in love with
Her heavenly bridegroom daily
Maybe she was attending her own masquerade
Was she hopeless?
Could any one of her own ambitions
Keep her from seeing the possibilities
God would place in front of her?

She screams silently
She catches her breath
Only to see the sun setting
And her reflection fading
In the darkness
Expecting God would give her
A sign with bright, flashing lights
She knows the truth
Of her heart's desires
Yes, she loved her work
Her sport
The life God had given her
Still, her heart yearned
To be an educated
Bride of Christ, Christian athlete
Teacher, friend, servant
Wife, mother, daughter
Tears rolled down her face
As she crossed the state line
Thinking how she's piled behind it all

Can You Give Me a Manual, Please?

I wish I could be handed a manual
Of all your plans and expectations of me
Every day I wish you could tell me
Exactly what you need me to know
What my purpose is
And what you want from me.

Sometimes I feel so lost
In this world
Amongst the sea of faces
Hiding behind their masks.

Life would be easier
If you could just provide us
With a playbook
So we're ready to face
Anything headstrong, armor and all
Always ready to make that move
Being completely fearless
Not having to stay on our toes.

Right now it's all a confusing mess
Playing the waiting game
Having to be extremely patient
Letting you be in control
Not knowing what's going to happen
No clarity or understanding
Why can't you give me a manual, script, or playbook?

Things would be so much easier
Simple and less confusing
No one would have to explain themselves
No more mysteries to be solved

All the books opened
Read cover to cover
Plays played out fully
Everyone would be a winner
In the crazy sea of life
No more need for masks.

Are You Reading the Story Cover to Cover?

We all are observers in this world
We each choose to see things from a certain perspective
Many choose to go with the flow
Viewing the popular perspective
Instead of their own
Or the one their heart and God is encouraging us
To view, understand, and accept

From a young age
We are told
"You never really know a story
Until you read it cover to cover"
We may never end up picking up a book
Reading it page by page
Comprehending the text
Becoming entranced by the mystery
And falling in love with the truth
The beauty and the realism of the story

So many miss the truth and beauty
Thanks to prejudgments
Picking up a copy of Spark Notes
However, that really does allow you to
Know the real story
But are you seeing the real pieces of the puzzle
Or just seeing what's on the surface

To be blinded by your own submissions
Is to possibly miss something amazing
For every story has a mystery to be revealed
Secrets to be understood and to be shared
All to be cherished

Beauty and grace to be captivated by
Nobility, and courage to respect and honor
Memories to be created
And blessings to last you a lifetime

Thoughts in a Box

She sits at her desk
Listens to the music play
Observes the patrons
As she folds towels

Her mind begins to ponder
The wonderful words of wisdom
Recently given to her
She realizes it's time

Time to open Pandora's Box
And place the events from the past days
As well as her thoughts into her box

For she knows she has two weeks
To put things aside
Forget about coworkers and drama
Realize what her priorities are in life

To an extent
Putting her thoughts in a box
Is a mini vacation from the Island and life

All she knows
She has to take
Those lessons she's been given
Use them in everyday life

Grow from it
And displace all those fears and doubts
While her thoughts are in a box!

Grand Masquerade of Life

Everything isn't always as it appears to be
Things may always appear to be one way
Yet when you look beyond the surface
There lies a greater mystery to be solved and unveiled

As time progresses
You soon learn there is so much more
To be learned than what is present
A part of you wants to be Sherlock Holmes and snoop
But in your heart
You know God's in control
Eventually you'll begin to see
The truth unmasked
And you're sticking to it

For so long, though
You've always believed
There wasn't much to see
However, at the right time
You were able to see past it all and understand
That behind the masquerade going on
There was so much to learn and share

Yes, it may all be a show
Being performed for all to see
Causing people to talk, stop, and stare
Letting speculation be known
Still, the mystery is solved

While patience and time are all we have
Little by little the mystery becomes known
Even if it is being conducted
Slowly, privately, or mysteriously

The symphony plays magical music
As the chorus sings the beautiful notes
Dictated by God himself

Getting to see all the clarity
That has been hidden
Behind the masks worn
In the Grand Masquerade of Life
Making your own judgments
Seeing the beauty and heart
Surpassing the presentation of masks

Over time you'll be able to know
All the secrets and stories
That lie beyond the greatest mystery
You've been blessed to come to research
Somehow you've grown fond of, are entranced by
And can only look forward to see
What God shares next

Last Chance, Last Dance, All in the Distance

I realized today something that I didn't expect to remember
I realized the importance of the little things
For so long, we've been busy planning our lives and have forgotten what matters
I've realized that it doesn't matter that you're moving on
Learning to let go and make every moment count
It may seem that there are some things that appear to be unfinished
But I know that God knows it's finished and time to close that one chapter and be prepared for the next
There's been so much I've wanted to do, people to see, things to say
Yet I know God knows best
In my heart and mind
There's that one last dance I want to make
That one man whom I just wanted to tell thank you
Those people who made a difference in your life
And you really just want to express your gratitude
However, I know time's run out
It's a little too late to make things right
Tie up loose ends
Be honest with those who need honesty
And leave a legacy
So here's to taking that one last exam
Those last steps down a hallway and paths
You've walked for half a decade
And just live it as if you're taking
A vacation to someplace else
The worst part of the situation
Is I was blinded so much by goals and dreams
I failed to see what was right in front of me
Maybe I wasn't supposed to
It just breaks my heart that
I may never know
As someone once told me

Just know God is looking out for your best interest
And it wasn't meant to be
So where you are, whoever you are
Thank you for the last dance
That one last chance for the song to be heard
As the music plays in the distance
And for being my friend
I'll never forget it all
It'll be in my heart forever

Wake Up from This Dream (You Can't Change a Tiger's Stripes)

Look at the world we live in
We're supposed to be living the dream
The world around us
Letting us do what we want
Having complete and total freedom
But baby,
Let's face it—
We're not!
Have you stepped outside the walls and roads
That surround you and your elegant life
And realized that our worlds are
Far different from what you'd expect
Maybe this is me overrationalizing
But I'm ready to face the truth
And call the world's bluff
I may not, nor never be
Below that ideal size, 10/12
I may always remain
But I am not afraid to say
Just because I don't look the part
And may not please certain people
Doesn't mean I'm not going anywhere
With the life and education I have
I may get dirty looks and
Have to listen to people talk down
On the pleasantly plump
Who happily grace the world
But I know that deep down
I'm a good-hearted person
Who's full of confidence and grace
Even if that means
I have to walk away and

Draw a line between you and me I'm willing to take the stand
It's time for me to tell you
For three years
I've kept my mouth shut
Put up with trying to wear the mask
Remained cool and confident
Even when I wanted to call your bluff
But baby
I'm sorry to tell you
Sometimes you can't change a tiger's stripes
And you have to understand
I'll never fit in with your world
Or this ideal Americanized, socialized
Ideal American Dream
So let's face the facts
Call a truce
And wake up from this dream

Finding Out Who We Are

Throughout our lives
We're always trying to figure out
Who we really are
Constantly, we're struggling with
The many trials and tribulations we're thrown
Often, we see ourselves
With a lot of unexpected events
And the unexpected
Even when this does occur
It's happening for a reason
Through our life experiences
Our eyes become open
And we tend to see life
In a completely different perspective
So when life throws you
That wicked curveball
Or plants the most delicate and beautiful flowers
Don't be afraid to hit the ball
And stop to smell the blooming flowers
Just remember
We should never lose sight of our
Morals, values, and beliefs
These four gifts are something
That are as precious to us as life itself
We should never forget
Our dreams, ambitions, and goals
Short-term and lifelong
All of this is what makes us
Who we are
Use it to battle everything
But never be afraid to discover who you are
And all we should do
Is just embrace it and live life

Summer of 2007

I just got back today
Ready to face you
Strong enough to conquer all my fears
So I'm ready to tell you
That I've gotta move on
Leaving the man I once knew
And all the drama that followed
Back in the summer of 2007
Because I am ready for a change
Just waiting for the fall
To see what new leaves of life
Will turn over
Ready to focus on the woman I am
And what the world means to me
Putting you and me in the past
Never to forget you
Just letting go of you
I'm now living for today
Always ready
For what God throws my way!

No More Conforming to the Man

We need to learn to say
When are we done conforming to the MAN?
Is it after we believe
Spending thousands of dollars
Trying to surgically or physically change ourselves
Because we believe
That if we do this
The world around us
Will fully accept us
With no questions asked?
Has it ever occurred to us
That just maybe
If we gave in to the man
Made the changes
He wouldn't be happy with us still?
When are we going to have
The courage to tell him
Our lives are not worth
Undergoing the knives
Or are you suggesting
We pick up a pack of cigs
Light 'em up
So we'll feel light
Enough is enough
Let's just take a stand
NO MORE CONFORMING TO THE MAN!

All My Life

All my life
I've been able to
Hide from the world
My own worst fears
My own faults

All my life
I've been able to
Cover up
The truth about me
What lies on my heart
And my deepest thoughts

All my life
I've been able to
Rely on my own strength
My independence and experience

All my life
I've been this person
Who could serve up
All sorts of advice
On relationships and life

Tell these great stories
On and of love and life
In hopes of encouraging others
To live life to the fullest
And to never give up on love
Learning from a friend's experience

All my life
No one's been able to
See through me
Or see the truth behind my baby blues

All my life
I've only really had
One person who could
See the best in me
And the truth about me
Since then
No one has been able to see
Until now

So unexpectedly
Someone has taken their time
To actually observe me
Get to know me
Care and think about me
And to see who I really am
Yet hasn't shut me out

I've realized
All my life
I've been a Southern girl
Who's nothing but
A hopeless romantic
A sociable, involved
Outgoing, spirited storyteller

One that only hides
In her works and activities
Convincing herself
That this is all she should be doing
And what is for the best

Being able to
Escape her own fear
Of wanting to be in a relationship
Fearing the effects and desires of it
And avoiding having her heart broken

Just constantly dreaming
Of that fairy-tale storybook
Movie-like romantic relationship
Trying to wait for Mr. Right
Instead of living life

All my life
I never knew
Someone could
Ever really see
Into the depths of my baby blues
Seeing into my soul
To see who I really was

I Am but a Songbird

I am but a songbird
Flying this Earth solo
With a mended heart
Battered and scorned soul
Always afraid of
Letting people get close
Constantly flying away from
Anything that causes challenges and complications
Trying to avoid the real songbird
Longing to be presented to the public

I am but a songbird
Who longs to feel what
Many others feel and experience
To understand and feel
The beauty of one of God's greatest gifts
Love
To the passion behind a kiss
Finding that one sparrow
Who is her soul mate
And he needs no explanations
For he is her best friend

I am but a songbird
Who longs to sing her song
Telling the world
Because of her imperfections
She'd rather hide away
Deciding when to push people away
Especially when she's confused
And she understands why she's flying

I am but a songbird
Who realizes all the world is
Nothing but a stage
And we are all players in it
Yet when we're in disguise
We can be liberated
Having the capabilities of
Singing what's truly in our hearts

I am but a songbird
Simply longing
To meet a set of eyes
That can see my soul and eyes staring back
That no sooner do our eyes meet
We simply love

I am but a songbird
Longing to be noticed
By all the world
Seen for the beauty of her heart and soul
Not for her outer image

I am but a songbird
Who longs to be free from pain and anguish
Who longs to be complimented and have her call
Heard from a mile away
Asking for the world not to judge her

Mostly, I am but a songbird
Ready to let go of it all
To let her golden heart and kindness shine
Ready to live, love, and be fearless
Because she is brave, courageous, spiritual, and hopeful

Chapter 5

Trips to Texas and Other Places

All journeys have secret destinations of which the traveler is unaware.

—Martin Buber

Traveling

Texas is my home and where a lot of my inspiration is derived, just as when I have traveled. Travel can be defined as visiting places that may be considered out of this world. Each adventure we take while we are dreaming, imagining, and drifting off in to another place; is an unexpected journey.

Traveling the Sea of Lost and Confused

Every time
I look into his eyes
I find myself rolling with the tides of time
I drift off to this place of the unknown
Unable to know where I'm going
Only to know that the good Lord's my captain
All I can do is brace myself
Say a few prayers and hold on tight

I feel I'm traveling on the Sea of the Lost and Confused
When I'm with him
I want to help him
And tell him it's gonna be OK
But I don't know if he believes me, Lord
If he'd believe me when I tell him
I understand and I've been there
If only he'd give me the chance
To take my offer
And let me do God's work

As I drift off
Into the unknown
I don't have any lifelines
To rely on if I need help
I just have my faith and hope
In the Lord above
I'm not scared or afraid
I'm ready to embrace it all
And surrender

Each time I'm with him
I never expect the same feelings or reactions
I can't explain it in words, but

It feels so right
When I'm with him
In some odd and unexplainable way
And I could stay lost in a sea of blues forever
For I know the Lord's at work
For the Lord's at work

Lord, please let him see
As I roll onto the shore
That you've sent me to him
And he doesn't have to be
Traveling on the Sea of the Lost and Confused

He Was Her Muse

She closed her eyes
As the Boeing 737 took off for the over-two-hour flight
She began to realize that she was leaving
A place where she had been able to see
Her faith grow stronger, be tested, and move amazing mountains
she was facing
She really didn't want to leave a place
Some might call a place of sin, but
She called it a place where she was allowed to let herself go
To really be herself, realize what she wanted out of life
Realize where she wanted to go
No one may exactly understand what she was experiencing
But she never really expected anyone to understand
She just wanted the world to understand
That every place you visit, travel to, or hear about
Has two sides
Never in a million years would she expect to understand
How it was possible to see the other side
Of a city many condemn and curse
Yet to her, she just embraced everything it had to offer
As she drifted off to sleep
She saw the silhouette of a man
A man whose touch she could remember
With the sound of his voice
The gentleness of his caring hands
And the love and spirit his arms provided
To this woman, this man was her muse
He inspired her in so many ways
He made her want to be a better person
Want to know the world more
Want to grow stronger in her faith
With him by her side
She knew that she could do anything

Regardless of what people told her
How is it
She could fear a man
Who would become her muse, her inspiration
Amazing how the power of one man's grace
Once embraced
Can touch the beating heart
Of a strong, loving, caring, spirited Southern belle
As she opened her eyes
And felt the plane land
She knew she was back in reality
However, she also knew
That this man she saw
Truly was her muse
Does Charming really exist?

Ride Back to the City

There she sits
Staring out at the tracks, waiting for the train
All she can do is pray, pray to God about how her heart is on fire
Yet shattering into a thousand tiny pieces
She knows she's doing his work and feels blessed
Sometimes the one person she can open up to without remorse seems silenced
She doesn't understand
She isn't afraid
She just needs honesty
She needs consistency
No tricks or lies
She knows her own heart, strengths, and passions
God, she needs clarity
None of this makes sense
This wasn't her
She can see the lights of the train in the distance
Time to stop worrying
She gets on board
Finds her seat and turns on her iPod
Panania bound
Time to put on her game face
She closes her eyes
Shuts off her emotions
And no matter how hard she prays he would come to his senses
She embraces the forty-minute ride
She gets off the train thanking God and ready to work
Each day is a gift

Waiting to Board a Flight to Neverland

Today's the day she's been awaiting
For the past several months
Finally, her chance to show everyone
She isn't afraid to overcome the odds
She couldn't believe she was
About to board a plane to Neverland
Face some of her biggest fears
All alone
With no one to hold her hand
Was she ready to fully do this?

She had already broken
The chains of her wounded heart
Showed she could surpass
Illnesses, injury, and negativity
Overcome much more than
Anyone would have expected
She discovered grace, forgiveness, and a new sense of being
Just reliving her passions
Nothing could weigh her spirits or drive her down

Despite the mistakes she'd made
She had learned from them
She had grown from them
Even slowly started to open
Her eyes and heart to
What God was presenting

The past twenty-four hours
Had seemed so surreal
None of it made sense
It all felt like a dream
God, what was going on?

Things were falling into place
In some odd way
Work was getting done
There really seemed
Like there was no division occurring
Amongst the people in the land

Even the King and his men
Held a different attitude and spirit
Towards the servants and those not of high class
It was startling

As she ran into the King
That previous morning
She felt she didn't know him
No matter the mockery
Heard in the background from his men
He gave her his undivided attention
What had she done to deserve this
Was the King she knew coming back?

About eighteen hours before her flight
She met with the King
On official business
Though she didn't want to
Have to write the story nor have this meeting
She knew God had his plan
The hysterical side of it
Was the date of the meeting

Twenty-six years prior
Her parents had been united in holy matrimony
And her grandfather went dancing with the angels
How much more ironic could things get?

After the meeting was over
Neither departed
They stayed engrossed in conversation

Maybe this was the way
It was meant to be all along
She was able to
Express many words of honesty
Straight from the heart to him

She also felt the man
She once knew and wanted to know
Was there right in front of her
Sitting across from her
Enjoying her company
As she enjoyed his

At one point in time
She glanced into his stained-glass sapphires
And could actually see her eyes
Staring back at her
She was speechless
Without thought
And could only think
God was in control
None of this added up

Somehow it seemed
All the air had been cleared
Time could only tell
One would hope
When the two departed
There seemed to be something
New or different in the air
And between the King and servant
Maybe the two did understand each other

All she knew was
She was at peace
And completely content
With things in her life
Happy exactly where she was

Nor would she change
A thing about it

"Hello, girl. Wake up. Get a grip"
That's all she kept thinking
She needed to be pinched
Smacked with a frying pan
Brought back down to Earth

While she sat on a plane
Waiting to go nineteen thousand feet into the clear blue sky
Nothing made sense to her anymore
It appeared she had been blessed
Blessed with some gifts, angels, and a beautiful life
She didn't feel she deserved
She wasn't anyone special
All she was
Was a servant
Taking a second chance
Living with no regrets
Going after her dreams
And answering God's call

"Passengers, at this time
The captain has turned on the *Fasten Seat Belts* sign
And the cabin door has been closed."

Take off
Off to Neverland!

Sunday Morning Sunrise

As the sun rises around 6:00 AM
The cool sea breeze
Fills the air with tranquility
To see the sun's rays
Dance upon the sea before me
I can see the sea
Sparkle like blue sapphires
I slowly close my eyes
To capture this picture
In my mind
To remind me of its beauty
I slowly open my eyes
With a delightful smile
Feeling the cool breeze
Stroke my soft skin
Sending chills throughout my body
Only to think of how much
This moment makes me feel
Truly happy
And reminds my heart to feel
What it's like when you're in love
The warmth, the passion, the comfort, the security
I slowly remove
My cold yet loving hand out of my pocket
Reaching out for your hand
Sadly, only to find you're not there
My smile drops and my heart aches
Oh, how I yearn to have
Your body next to mine
And your hand reaching out
Entwined with my hand
Enjoying and celebrating
And cherishing this moment

How I long to know
That feeling again
As the glowing sun fully rises
All I can do is
Close my eyes
And imagine you beside me
Your soft voice, angelic smile
And bold and boundless breathtaking eyes
Soaking up the sun
Enjoying the cool breeze
Just you and I
Together, alas
This is our never-ending moment
Wait . . .
The alarm on my phone goes off
Abruptly
My heart is reminded
That no matter how far apart
We are
You're always with me
And I with you
For at the dawn of
Each new sunrise
Forevermore
I remain yours
Always

A Clear, Starry Texas Night

On a starry Texas night
Underneath a clear, moonlit sky
That only God could have created
So beautiful and perfectly in his image
Surrounded by God's creations
Away from civilization
No one judging
No one watching
A place where you can be
As free as the jennie
Singing in that singsong
I don't believe
Anyone could have predicted
The amazing things that happened

During that forty-hour trip
Escaping reality and society
While the night wound down
When it was time to head back
To our cabins for a slumber
Something in the air
Became sweet
Even if a face cannot be remembered
The melodies heard in the night can
It was an unexpected blessing
An unanswered prayer
A secret desire fulfilled
Here was a Southern girl
So in tune with her relationship with God and Christ
Who always wondered
Even if it was a sign of mere friendliness
Or even a kind joke

To hear a man sing a sweet song
Serenading her
Biding her a sweet ado
Although she may not
Be able to remember the face of the singer
She'll always remember how his song
Was a bittersweet way
To end the most life-changing day
What he may never know is
A simple, sweet serenade
Had never happened to her
In the almost twenty-three years of life
She has been blessed with
Thus why she sang back
Man-hating Carrie Underwood songs
His act of kindness
Truly will be
Something that she'll never forget
Even if she can't remember his face
His song sent her into a trance
A trance she had only
Dreamed or written about
A trance that allowed her to open her eyes
To understand that
Friendly and kind people still exist in this crazed world
Regardless if their paths may never cross again
She'll never forget him or his song
The smile on his face and how the moonlight
Allowed the light to shine in his eyes
Knowing that for at least one moment
There was a man with a heart bigger than the state of Texas
She can only hope and pray
The image of the man
Who serenaded her
That spring night away from reality
Performing a small yet meaningful
Random act of kindness

Will reappear in her mind
But for now
She'll never forget the songs
And always hear them playing
In memory of a starry Texas night!

Reflections of a Small Town

Driving down that lonely two-lane highway
To a small town near San Antone
Just where US Highway 87 meets Texas Highway 123
It's typically a small, sleepy little town
However, if you're ever around
On the third weekend of June
Every year, you'll see the town
Turned upside down

It's been three years
Since she's been back home
To experience what the town's known for
She'd always had something going on
That would stop her from making it back

She had no expectations
She was excited
To finally be able to
Bring out those old blue jeans
That straw cowboy hat
And of course her flip-flops
Y'all have to remember she's
Truly a "country girl," with a touch of the Island

There was no doubt in her mind she was
That all-American small-town country girl
She had no shame in who she was
Where she came from
And everything that came along with that territory
However, she did realize one thing

Walking onto the grounds
She never would imagine running into
So many people she once called friend
Completely in another world
They were either drunk
Or very close to it

She couldn't believe how these people she
Thought were her friends
Had truly changed over the years
Their attitudes and personalities
Almost as if
The people they once seemed to be
No longer existed
It had all been an act

She noticed how people
Walked around with beer in their hands
Those fake smiles
And their party-like side
These were people she didn't want to be around
Not to mention, bugging her about her single life

Her nature wasn't living up to
The small-town life expectations
She didn't feel that she had to
Follow through with that lifestyle

While she was there
She vividly remembered
Why she never would forget
Her former classmates and what they were like
She never really fit in with them
She always was living her dreams
She never let anything get to her

She stood on the pavilion
Listening to Gabe Garcia
Not only enjoying the country music
But also his inspirational words
To never let go of your dreams
And always follow them

After the celebration was over
She began to realize
She loved going home because of the people
Not the people she went to school with
They mattered, but they didn't influence her

However, she did realize that
She didn't want to be like them
She wanted to live out her dreams
Never stop in between
Get her three degrees
Never let up until
She had that PhD in her hands

Not saying she was better than anyone else
She knew she was just the same as anyone
But she knew she wanted to be
That small-town All-American girl
Who didn't change who she was
Once she turned the legal drinking age

She didn't want to let that alcohol
Solve her problems
She wanted to make sure
She made the difference she knew she could
And never lost sight of who she was
Who she could become
And she was going to be

Most notably
She never forgets
When she drives back down that
Two-lane highway back to the Island
A place she knows where her heart belongs
To the place where she can be free
And continue to still be herself
Following her dreams
Always believing everything is possible

Without Looking Back

She sat quietly in the airport terminal
Waiting for her flight to board
For almost six weeks now
She had been looking forward
To being able to escape the Island
Get out of Texas
And go out West

Many thought she was insane
When she had first
Mentioned her desire
To fly out to Denver for the Fourth

The timing wasn't the greatest
But for a while
She'd had a feeling
She was going to need this trip

It wasn't until
Trouble entered her life
That she knew her truest reasons
For the significance of going to Denver

The trip was going to help her
Be able to find herself (so to speak)
Just being able to get away
Put Summer I's drama behind her
And look ahead
Without turning back

She would only hold
The important details
Of Summer I in her heart

Like the friendships created
And the wonderful memories
She would always share with others

She couldn't wait
To land in the Mile-High City
Hopefully to see her Bubbie and future adoptive sister-in-law
Waiting to greet her
And get to hear about the exciting adventure
Those two had conjured up

Since day one she had put those two in charge
And certainly had no expectations of the trip
She'd dubbed the happy couple
Her travel guide and director for her Independence weekend

For once on a trip
She didn't care about having an itinerary
She longed for something different
Something full of thrills and excitement
Something unforgettable

In a few short hours
All her secret little wishes
Would hopefully begin to come true
Having that in mind
Her heart began to leap for joy
At the thought of it all

Ah, no more trouble
Or her wonderful work family
Constantly encouraging her to believe
That Trouble was the one for her

Six AM—boarding time
Her heart raced
Her stomach turned with butterflies
And her mind began to spin

What in the world was she doing
About to board a plane to Denver
A week before nationals
When she should be in training
Or spending the Fourth of July with her family

As she stepped on the plane
While the flight attendant greeted her
It all hit her
She knew it *exactly*
What she was doing

She was going out West
To clear her mind
Spend time with Bub and Angel
Get exposed to a different part of the country
Forget about everything
Come to her senses
Relax, unwind
Become 100 % mentally prepared
For the upcoming competitions on the D-Tour

Nope, she was not psychotic
Taking time out for herself
Although the timing may not have been perfect
Nothing ever really is
She wanted to become
A healthy and mentally prepared athlete

She made her way
To the back of the plane
Found her seat
Buckled up and
Prepared for takeoff

As the plane made its way
Down the runway of San Antonio International
For takeoff to Denver

A sweet smile appeared on her face
For in only a few short hours
She'd be out West
In a different time zone and state
More ready than she had ever been for anything
To see what was in store for her
Without looking back

Trip Out West

The drive to the airport
Was full of silence and complete emotions
She couldn't believe that
Her vacation was ending

In a few short hours
She'd be back in another time zone and state
And soon be back on the Island
Back to training
Getting ready for nationals
And the possibilities of
Seeing someone
She had no desire to see
Only to try to let go
Before anything got to crazy
And salvage the friendship

Her mind had become clear
She had been able to relax and unwind
Let loose for a while
She didn't worry about anything
Let her tour guides have complete control
Guiding her on an unforgettable, awesome adventure
She definitely knew
She would never forget
Her trip out West
And all the amazing discoveries she had made
Both mentally and physically
No one could explain it all

Oh, how she longed
For her adventure and vacation

Not to come to an end
It was amazing and unforgettable

The only few things
She looked forward to doing
Were getting to tell her
Adoptive family and BFF at work
All about what she'd been able to experience
And seeing the people she had missed
On her trip out West

Besides missing people
And getting back to training
She couldn't have cared less about
Getting back on the Island
Knowing she'd chosen to let things go
And not looking back

Being carefree and stress-free
Sleeping in and living
Seeing places she'd only read or heard about
From the Mountains to an unforgettable Rockies game
Getting to bond with Bubbie and meeting his other half
Seeing the Castle in the Sky
Dancing and singing in a snow flurry
At fourteen thousand feet above sea level
To experience Downtown Denver and Red Rocks

At this point in time
She'd been able to be free
And unafraid to try new things
All while meeting a stranger
Who could be her future adoptive sister-in-law
And spending that time with her Bubbie
Nothing could top
The feelings and these present emotions

However
She couldn't lie to herself
She had been presented with a few challenges
And learned to grasp a better understanding
Of so many things
Such as culture and relationships
She was also a witness
To see how God could work in mysterious ways
Throwing so many curveballs
And where hitting them takes us

As she sat besides
A sweet, loving couple
She loved and admired
Her mind began to wonder and consider
What she had been told at dinner the night before

They told her how life
Can have so many unexpected twists and turns
And if you're not prepared
You may completely strike out or miss things

Sometimes we may never know
Or understand what God's plan is
But you have to be a little prepared
It's great having goals and dreams
Yet a part of you
Has to consider the idea of a relationship
Somewhere in your life and down the road

There she sat
Completely puzzled and speechless
She had no idea
How to respond to their comments
Never before had anyone
Confronted her with such a situation

She did not want to agree
With anything they said
She wanted to sit there
Literally in denial
Not think about him
That cold block of ice
Who caused trouble
For half the time
She hated him
And half the time
She loved him
That was the purpose of coming out West
Place her problems and issues behind her
Never to look back
Still a part of her
Longed to see him again
To hear his corky voice
Gaze into his blissful and boundless blues
To hear his amazing voice sing to her
As well as duet with him
To feel the warmth of his bear hugs
Hear the beat of his heart
And see that sweet Southern smile

She couldn't help
But to learn to face the reality
She knew what her heart
Was trying to tell her at the table
Secretly, she didn't hate him
Nor did she have a problem with him

Much to everyone's surprise
They'd be pretty shocked to know
The one who tended to be her problem and challenge her
Simply met the characteristics
Of a man she never expected to exist
This man was only a dream

The longer the couple
Engaged in this conversation
The more her heart wanted to scream
"This man wasn't supposed to exist
And do so many things he had
Nor was he supposed to be
Encouraging her to open her eyes
To see the possibilities"

The longer the night carried on
She was capable of seeing
The couple's unconditional love for each other
The more she secretly prayed
She'd know the feeling of what she was witnessing
And wondered why a dawn of a new day
Flashed in front of her and lingered in her heart

Was the couple supposed to guide her
To keep an open mind and heart
And wait patiently for everything to pan out
Just as her adoptive big brother had once said
And maybe that dreams do exist

She didn't know what to think
So she slept on it
Tried to forget about the dinner conversation
And not let it ruin her last hours
Of her unforgettable trip out West

During the drive to the last site on the trip
Discussion of marriage and the future
Seemed to occur and be unexplainable

She tried to sit in the passenger's seat
And not think of the subject
Even though secretly
She longed and dreamed of it

To her Bub
She was just silent

To him, though
He had the faith
That one day she'd get married
Raise a family
Be the ideal wife and teacher
As she touched the lives of others
Not end up going alone and living with cats

Through his words
He tended to express
His concern and love for her
He didn't want her to give up
On love nor give up hope

Just let this man
She didn't want to publicly consider
Come around and allow himself
To realize the truth and how he felt
Don't hide from him or push him away

For her Bub had faith
That this time around
He knew she'd truly meet someone
Who was the right guy for her
He just begged her not
To really walk out on him
Or do anything she'd regret

On the last day of her trip out West
She didn't want to even have the Hulk-like man
Enter her thoughts
But for some odd reason
The couple felt this guy was something

They presented her with options
To only encourage her
Just not to give up on the possibilities
That anything can happen

For her to hear this
Was mind-boggling
Because she had never felt
The way she currently did
Nor been in this type of situation
What was she going to do?

They slowly pulled into Denver's airport
To the departure drop-off
She tried not to think
About her adventure ending
Nor leaving the couple

The only thing that gave her hope
Was the vivid rainbow
That appeared in the sky
Even as they assisted her with her luggage
And said their farewells
She tried not to cry
She forced herself to barely shed a tear
Just focusing on the beauty of the rainbow

For once she entered the airport
She knew in a few hours
It'd all be over
But without looking back
She'd never forget the
Wonderful memories and adventure
Of her trip out West

Chapter 6

Heartbreak and Healing

Healing takes courage, and we all have courage, even if we have to dig a little to find it.

—Tori Amos

About Healing and Heartbreak

We all have had our own share of heartbreaks and gone through our own experiences of healing. The healing begins with having the courage to learn through every heartbreak. Sometimes heartbreak can send us down a dark path. Other times it opens our eyes, sending us on a path of self-discovery. Always, we can share our experiences with others.

Live and Let Love

Driving down
That one-lane Texas highway
On another Sunny afternoon
Is something I've always enjoyed
Seeing the wide open spaces
Of the countryside
Often wondering where it leads to
Thinking of what it'd feel like
To journey to the unknown
And to never return
Flying free like a butterfly
As I turned my eyes
Back to the endless one-lane highway
Something so marvelous caught my eye
For the first time I saw
These colorful patches of
Beautiful and delicate Texas wildflowers
Indicating that spring was here
A new season and a time for change
Noticing the flowers
Brought a sweet smile to my face
Something I hadn't done in very long time
Suddenly
A sense of radiance and joy came over me
Not only could I feel that
Spring was truly here, but
For the first time
Since Sam's death two years ago
I felt I was finally ready to let go
Of all my fears and anger
Allow myself to want to experience
What if feels like to be happy and in love
Able to be myself

And let someone get to know me
To be able to live and let love
When I arrived at my destination
Not only had two hours passed
I realized that today was
The second anniversary of Sam's death
And the day that I knew I was finally ready
To no longer live in fear but
To live and let love.

The Crimes I Have to Pay For

For years I've had to hold on
To those terrible little secrets
Which have left me
Mentally and emotionally scarred
You've said you were sorry
And I've forgiven you
Brushed it off
Walked on tall
Not letting the world know
I'm living proof
Of your hurtful wounds
My heart aches when we're together
I gaze into your eyes and I see it
I see your guilt
Your shame
But it doesn't mean
A dang thing to you
Everyone thinks you're so great and perfect
Completely not capable of
Mentally and emotionally abusing anyone
But you know it's all
Just a plain act
We both know your crimes
Which you should be charged with
You're guilty as sin
I'm the one
Who's broken and angry
Yet I must keep my lips sealed
And go to my grave with it
So many times
I've had the motive
To spout my mouth off
Save my soul

Rid myself of my shame
Slowly let my wounds heal
No longer feel as if
I am angry and scorned
Able to fly and see again
Let's face it
Love is blind and crazy
I'm sworn to secrecy
Acting like nothing's happened
Living in our lie
And for you
You're the one
Who's everyone's respectable hero
People bowing down, humbling
Showing gratification
When the crowds gather around
As your parade goes by
Waving your colors grandly
I have to smile in shame
Acting normal, innocent, and humbled
Simply obliging you
Seeing your love embracing you
But for once in your life
To erase what you've done
I'd love for you
To show *me* homage
Fix your mistake
Take away my pain
Let me have a full heart
Able to love fully
Have a normal, grand, jubilant life
To have all the same things and more as you
Coming out as a hero and champion
But let's be real
You're always going to be
The all-star and MVP
People loving you
Getting everything you want

Never realizing
There's someone walking around
Suffering from your abuse
With scars and wounds
Having to pay for your crimes!

The Silence: The Truth That Can Set You Free

It's past time when we have to look back
Realize things should become
Water under the bridge
For so long I had this desire
This burning desire to tell
How much I was in love with you at one time
And I possibly could still be
But then it hit me
God knew why the two of us
Weren't suppose to meet up
When I traveled up north
Because he knew that the truth
Would have led us to unhappiness
I never would have understood
Why not being honest with you
Drove me up a wall
However, it is my love and faith in God
That allowed me to understand
That silence can occur for a positive reason
To have told you the truth
Would have been drifting down a path
A path that you and I have both surpassed
The truth wouldn't have set us free
Indirectly, I believe, the truth
The truth would have been the death of us
But now here I stand
Less than seventy-two hours from being twenty-three
To openly admit to you
That yes, I may love you
Yes, I will always love you, my dear brother in Christ
Yet I know in my heart
Us being apart is for the best
Just know I'll always love you

And be here for you like a sibling should
But sometimes I believe
You and I are better this way
Maybe one day, it'll change
For now, I know
Moving on from you may be hard
But it's for the best
You're happy and that's the greatest thing
I could ever see happen for you
I know one day, I'll be 110 percent happy
And understand the expression
Two halves are better than one
For now
I'm enjoying this path I'm on
Growing a little stronger each day
Not yearning for lustful things
Or what'd it be like no longer being single
Or to know what it'd be like
To caress the lips of a man for the first time
I'm just enjoying striving to be me
Living it up with no temptations
Or those little worries of tomorrow
Just seeing where this God-given path
Is going to lead me next
Enjoy your happiness
And understand silence is for the best
And know the silent truth
Can set you free

Memories of a Lesson I'll Never Forget

A part of me
Just like everyone else
Probably wishes for one more day
One more hour
One more minute with
That person or people
Who have touched my life

Sometimes I feel I've been so blinded
By my own drive for
A closer relationship with my father
And continue falling back in love with Christ

I feel that I was somewhat naive
And unable to see what was right in front of me
Fully embracing the lesson
And time with the person teaching me

Although I might not ever
Cross the path of one of my teachers
Who showed me
That I needed to let my pride go
And it wasn't all about winning the tangible prize
The prize can often be
Finishing the race
Getting back up when you fall
And always glorifying God

To this teacher
You may never know the lesson
That you taught me in less than forty hours
But I thank you and only hope

That one day I'll be able to
Return the favor

Just know
I'll never forget the kindness and care you displayed
When I had the opportunity to be embraced
With your gentle presence
And see the size of your gentle heart
Which is bigger than the Lone Star State

Thank you for teaching me
And serving our Heavenly Father
May you continue
Touching the lives of the people you meet
And never stop
Serving, coaching, and being the blessed person you are

Who knows
Maybe one day
We'll have the opportunity
For our paths to cross
Until then
I'll never forget you and the memories
I have of you

Right Direction

I close my eyes
And drift to the place where
Complete peace and serenity has occurred
A place where God's love and grace is everywhere
I start to see the faces of those
Who have inspired me and touched my life
Helped me realize that one person can be
A complete game changer
And that miracles happen every single day
As I see the images of those faces
I find myself only being able to see
The eyes of one man
Very soft, pleasant, comforting
Caring, and most importantly, serving
I can hear his voice
And the song he is always singing
The words that he spoke
So soft, yet so innocently
A part of my heart
Simply yearns to one day
Be able to find the owner
Of the man with the soft eyes
Singing and praising our Heavenly Father
I sit back
Take a breath
And pray that one day
God will give me the opportunity
To come into contact
With the owner of those eyes and that song
I know one day
I'll be given the right directions
And things will be
Back like they were

When all of us
Were in the place of serenity
It rightly doesn't matter
If I can't remember
The owner of those soft eyes
Who just had a way of singing
I just know that
God placed these people
In my life
And they taught me unforgettable lessons!

Letting Go

I don't know how it happened
But unfortunately it did
For the longest time
I knew I had feelings for you
However, I got this thought
And realized that I had feelings
For another man, too
As time went on
I soon felt torn in two directions
And noticed that we grew distant
You didn't seem like
The same man I fell in love with
(Little did you know I was)
You seemed to just want to avoid me
I began to notice something
That there was a man
Who gave me hope and life
And accepted me for who I was
Who had always been there, but
I could never see it until now
Three weeks soon passed
Not a word from you
Only avoidance from you
Reality set in
A curveball smacked me
Like a flash of lightning
My eyes were opened
And I could feel happiness and newness
My heart was pulling in a new direction
On one cool December night
Truth was revealed
I had a decision to make
This other man had me test myself

Just stop thinking and just live life
For once in my life be myself and
See who I really was
Just as he saw me
And think about what path of life I wanted to choose
Also to be sure I wanted to go down that path
No turning back no matter what
Suddenly I could see how happy I was and free
Days had gone by since I was presented with a choice
I saw you and I knew I had to know
That my feelings for you were no longer there
And that I knew the free and spirited path was
The path I could hear the music down
When I saw you I got the same old feelings
And I wanted to avoid them, but I couldn't
So I waltzed right by you
And we spoke kindly
Just like we had done in the past
However, that spark wasn't there
Nor could I hear the music
After you congratulated me
And we said our farewells
I knew at that moment
Exactly where my heart was guiding me
Now I don't know why
Or how it will all turn out
But I do know
I'm just going with the flow
And living *mi vida loca*!

I'm Running from You

They ask me what I'm running from
I simply respond, "Nothing"
Yet deep down I long to respond
With a simple three letter word—Y-O-U
Why Y-O-U
Is fairly easy to explain
If you could really see beyond
My sea of baby blues and read my mind
You could understand
And see why I'm running
I don't dwell on the past
I only reflect and learn from it
A long time ago
I learned not to bring
Personal feelings and emotions
Into the professional realm
Therefore, I see it's in the best interest
To run from my feelings inside
I've learned to have that wall up
So I'm more likely not to fall
We all make mistakes
And learn from them
This time around, running from you
Was the best thing I could do
Keep that wall up
Watch my bounds
And only seek the lines I can cross
Not running into a lake
But only running from Y-O-U.

A New Change of Heart

The alarm went off around six AM
She got up, got dressed, went to practice
As she got back about two hours later
She suddenly realized exactly what
She truly wanted
Frustration abruptly came upon her
She stopped dead in her tracks
Sat down at the table
And began working on homework

Little did she know
At this exact moment in time
Her life was about
To undergo a revolution
Throughout the day
She was in nothing
But a complete *daze*
By the end of the day
She realized that
Silently, she was going to
Be able to let go of some "extra" baggage

She woke up the next morning
In nothing but a complete glow
Like a new person
So full of life and happiness
Her confidence had been
Fused and restored
Mostly knowing that
No man was going
To control her and
Overpower her own thoughts

At this point
She realized
She was ready to
Walk into a room
And be able to own it
And then conquer the world

All she could believe
Was that God had finally spoken to her
Allowing her to see
That he truly does work in
Mysterious ways

"Trust in the Lord
For he truly knows what is in store for your destiny."

Chapter 7

Land Down Under

She had to leave the comfort of Texas and go into the unknown in the land down under. What she discovered in Australia was wonderful. What she discovered was herself and her passions; having her heart split between the deep blue skies of Texas, and the culture and life of Sydney and Australia.

—J. Ko

Traveling to Australia and becoming immersed in the culture, my life was forever changed. At first, many thought I was crazy for going, but it was not their choice. The three months I spent alone in Sydney gave me an opportunity to find myself—as a person and an athlete. Upon passing through customs at the Sydney airport, I realized I was leaving part of my heart there and going back to the other half of my heart. Ultimately, I wanted the opportunity to share my growing experiences with you.

Half My Heart in Down Under

She gazed out the window
Looking at Botany Bay one last time
She couldn't believe her time
To return from halfway around the world
Had already come
It seemed like only yesterday
Some of her dreams were coming true
Right in front of her eyes
As she saw a glimpse of the city
And the pilot said, "Lift off"

Tears rolled down her face
And she prayed
"God, I feel like I've been livin'
In a completely surreal state of being
Yet all I can think of is how I'm not
Good with good-byes
All I wanted to say before I got on the lift
Was 'I'll never forget you
You'll always be in my heart
I, too, really hope we meet again'
But I froze, left a note
Got on the lift
Realizing I had just left
Half my heart Down Under
(Yeah, half my heart)"

When it all began
She knew it'd be an adventure
An opportunity
A small-town girl
Could put on her bucket list
Never would she have expected

To see what the other half
Of the world had to offer again
Still, she could believe the bliss
So sensual and magical

Time was passing by
Emotions shaken, rattled
Her heart pulled
She never really planned
To find herself and know who she was
Her passion, faith, desires
All in complete harmony
How could it be
Oh, tell the world how could it be
Yeah

Out of her bag fell a card and a passport
She read the card thinking
How she touched lives
And how they touched hers
Then she found an address
She closed her eyes
Oh . . .

Her mind raced
Thinking of a man she had met unexpectedly
The laughs, chats, little moments
So rare, natural, real
All unheard of
Never once realizing the time
Which passed by
How could she forget a kind and gentle face
And those dark earnest eyes
Finally, in the twenty-five years on this earth
She wore no mask
She was her true self
How could he notice her out of a crowded room
For whatever reason

Every moment priceless and unforgettable
In the end, no barriers
God, explain

Plane lands
Voice on the PA says
"Welcome to the USA"
She would never change a thing, yeah . . .

Dancin' Matilda's Waltz

There she stood, swaying to "Matilda's Waltz."
A part of her wondered
What it would be like to sing with the singer that night.
Then she said
"I know God has my road mapped out for me, and
Maybe my voice isn't meant to
Be heard this way. Oh, no.
It's not meant to be heard on a public stage."

She sighed and prayed while swaying to the beat of "Matilda's Waltz"
"God, just show me your will for me and I'll go, yes, Papa.
I've served you all my life so far
Could you show me where I'm supposed to go
On this broken road I've been traveling on
I know it's blessed and full of hope and love
Yet a part of me believes I'll never have my chance
To be out there on the dance floor
Smilin' away, dancin' away, with no worries
To 'Matilda's Waltz.'"

As the band played on
She could only dream
One day her prince would find her
Ask her to dance.
When their eyes met
He'd know she was the one he was meant to be with
The one he had been praying for all his life.
They'd danced as Matilda's melody played on
As if only they and God existed.
What a moment
Yeah, what a moment it'd be.

She just smiled
Maybe he was an illusion, a dream, a bittersweet thought.
God needed to give her clarity.
She wanted to see parts of the world.
Who knew, maybe changing it
With one song or by touching one child's life at a time
How could she have it all.
The world still knew little about her.
Papa, a little help, please.

As she watched people dancing around her, she gazed in wonderment.
Someday, soon, she hoped
She'd be hearing this waltz play
While her parents danced in delight
The room filled with mystic and passion
Laughter expressed
She and God's charming getting to explore
A not-so-broken road
Exploring the world and touching lives
Erasing the marks of the past
As she closed her eyes.

So maybe this is all a fairy tale, but a girl can dream.

Thousands of Miles from Home

Thousands of miles from home
She stares out the window
Of the train taking her from the country to the city
She constantly wonders
How she could have ended up
At a place she feels at home

She's praying to God
Thanking him
For the life she's been given
Letting her see her dreams come true
Bring her back to a place she could be herself
Not worry about anything
Not feel the world judging her
Or the other anxieties of life
Still, deep down she's praying even deeper
For some clarity and not thinking about
Who she left behind

It's been a few days
Since she's heard from him
Still she doesn't even know
How he feels about her
She's tired of not being able to express herself
Letting him know what's on her heart
Telling him how he makes her feel
All she wants to tell him
Is she needs his support, friendship, and understanding
None of this is about something more
But what does it matter
Talking to him is like talking to a wall

She sits back in her seat
Riding along, listening to her iPod
Trying to not cry
Watching the fellow passengers
Board the trains, read the paper, or mess with technical gadgets
She hopes none of them notice the tears in her eyes
She tries not to cry or find something to break
She wants to try not forgetting about the time out of the city

The time she spent out in the city
Made her forget about him
Made her forget about the fury of city life
And about the worries that often bother in the office
Sometimes, though
She found herself a little homesick
But knew her family was a call a way
And she put her faith in God

No matter what she did
She couldn't seem to get that man
Who had baffled her heart
And her mind
As her train neared Central Station
If only God could show her his plan
Show her how it didn't make sense
How it could be great one moment
Then extremely distant the next
All she wanted to do was sleep at night
God, please help her, she begged
"Central Station," the conductor said
There was nothing else she could do

Chapter 8

Heart and Soul

Doing things the way you see it, going by your own heart and soul that is pure artistic integrity.

—Lars Ulrich

Each of us has a heart, and we each have a soul. Many times, our hearts are glowing and our souls are on fire. Often our hearts and souls can create beautiful pictures.

Stealing a Darkening and Icy Soul

For so long I believed
My soul was nothing
But dark, vindictive, manipulative
And my heart was as icy
As the glaciers of Antarctica
I felt completely frozen and evil
The thought of life or light
Breaking through the emptiness
Of my blackened, emotionless heart and soul
Was completely unthinkable, silent, and faint
Never in a million years
Did I ever expect the unexpected
To happen to me
I expected to become
Completely vindicated and mesmerized
Until you walked into my life
It's strange to see
How from the moment the door flung open
And I started to get to know you
That you completely touched my heart and soul
I feel as if I can start to believe
You've stolen my heart
By the way you've moved me
Even if I can appear
To be set in my mischievous ways
I am starting to feel and be strong
Funny how now I yearn
For your sincere, sweet embrace
And I can't wait until I see you again
Regardless of what separates us
I know you've helped restore new hope in me
Helped me to see what I haven't

Been able to see for so long
Your warmth and life
Has completely captured
This ruptured, darkened, and icy soul

Love: God's Superpower

We constantly find ourselves traveling the very diverse world
Under the influences of the media, our culture, and even the demands of our society
Yet even when we see people changing
Our family and friends fighting a crazy cold war
The gifts from our heavenly Father still remain
Faith, hope, and love
Love being the most powerful and moving gift given
To be able to love
Isn't exactly the easiest task in the world
Many times we see people yearning for it
Yearning to understand it
We even seen relationships of all sorts
Crumbling left and right
However, when a person has the ability
To trust, to never give up, to hope, to understand
Real, true, enduring love can exist
They say that when you're in love
The feeling is so right
Everything makes complete sense
You feel like you've been given superpowers
Which allow you to do anything
When you're in love
It feels like all the craziness going on
Can be defeated because
You are not alone and you've finally
Found that one person
Sent to you
To help make it through anything
The ability to love with all your heart, mind, body, and soul
Is that superpower given from God
And a blessing in disguise

Waking Up Every Day

Every day I wake up
With a smile on my face
Every day is a new beginning
A day full of new breathtaking moments
And so many blessings
Every day is a day you save me
And each day I find myself
Falling deeper and deeper in love with you

Every day I feel you
Picking me up off the ground
Lending me a helping hand
Every day your hand
Has been able to take this hardened heart
And help it heal
With your gentle care, love, and compassion
Every day you've come around
When I feel completely beaten and stressed
Your words and actions
Are exactly what the doctor has called for

Every day I feel I'm on top of the world
I feel full of drive, power, confidence, and security
It seems your spoken words
Have become words of inspiration and comfort
Every day your presence in my life
Means more than you'll ever know
I know I can make it
I'm blessed and fearless
I am saved

Every day I can't stop smiling
I can't wait to see what happens next

Every day I know there's someone who understands
Who understands me and doesn't judge me
Every day I'm finding more reasons
Why I feel blessed you're in my life
And why I'm falling more in love with you

Every day I find myself in a state of bliss
Just to know how lucky I am
To be miles apart from you
And still feel ignited
Yet I can't wait to see you again
Every day I am me, and I am free

Casting a Spell at a Masquerade

You say you're cold and evil
Cruel and despicable
In a matter of time
Any female could be a part
Of your master conquest
Become captivated
Underneath your magical spell
A spell which the lucky female
Has cast upon her
She'll fall right into your trap
A trap wherein you might say
"Once she enters there's no turning back."

An outsider may not be able to
Foresee where the journey will go
But an insider can only fear
Fear that the madness
Doesn't control her or change her
Yet another can believe
You're only fooling yourself
It is impossible

As time changes
So can you and your vindictive ways
Your spell only sounds like a hoax
Maybe I'm the foolish observer
Who chooses to believe
That your spell is really
A hoax waiting to happen
Due to the obvious fact
That there is a greater power
In this world we live in

You may be consumed
In conquests and living up to your evilness
Thinking the intensity you bestow
From your psychic and mystic eyes
Can lure an audience member in
Given the appropriate amount of time
Slowly you'd make your move

But let me tell you this
Not this time
I've got you pegged
I feel you're going through a change
Even if you believe you're cold
And you've got an extreme hardened heart

Deep down inside of you
Is a man with a good soul
A soul that is warm, open, and soft
A man that doesn't mess with spells
Full of an evil spirit
A man through playing games

Between you and me and a fence post
All of this is just a charade
We're at a masquerade
And because you're still
Dealing with you and your plans
You're afraid to take the mask off
And stop casting and planning conquests
To be able to wake up
And see the great power of goodness
That constantly surrounds you

Maybe it is time
For you to swallow your fears and pride
Release all the evil
And no longer feel trapped

In the evil and cold world
You've been dancing in

I know what I see
What I've always seen
Will you ever see what I see
Or will the planes of time be broken
And all this time
I've been falling into your trap
Eventually being cast under your spell

The Heart's Hope

As the day went by
I tried to focus on
Everything and anything
But you
You were all I could think about
Distilled in my mind
Is how those boundless, bold eyes of yours
Seemed to contain fear and confusion
Something I never expected to see in them
Then again
I never expected
What happened to happen
To get into a quarrel
With the one person
I truly care for and about
And want to be with from here on
Even though I have
My own way of showing it
And I know truly cares for me
Looking into those
Mysterious dark eyes of yours
As we departed
Only made me realize
How much more
I didn't want to push you
Out of my life
But to keep you by my side
For eternity
Also to become more determined
To help you see
I'm not going anywhere
And willing to take a chance
On something that I know

Will be great
And will be good for the both of us
Sounds crazy, but I know
That when I'm with you
And you're with me
Everything's going to be all right
Nothing bad's going to happen
Only great things
I still hope
After what I did
You're still willing
To give me a chance
Just listen to your heart
I know I am to mine
Let the river run its course
All I know is
Just don't give up on true happiness
Give your heart a chance
And time will
Prove everything's meant to be

Hurricane Fire and Ice

The world around her
Is like a hurricane crashing onto shore
Allowing a whirlwind of chaos to follow
Water rising about twelve feet high
Her thoughts and emotions
Flood the stress in front of her
Nothing seems to make sense

As she steps outside
The wind is whipping fast
She is blown back inside the house
She is confused and frustrated
She wishes the wind
Would carry her out to the rapid sea
So she can drift away
To escape all the craziness
The storm has caused

Everything is falling to pieces
Windows being broken
Buildings being destroyed
The unexplainable is occurring
She's happy, scared, overwhelmed, stressed, and confused
All at the same time

How is it that the storm can make her
Overjoyed for four people she loves
Be inspired, motivated, and prioritized
Yet a certain event
Has her unable to speak and explain

While love and confusion appear
She is more determined to

Be carried out to the sea
This is so unlike her

As the water continues
To crash inland
Her desire to scream and cry strengthens

On her second attempt
To escape outside
To figure out what is going on
Fear, anxiety, confusion, the unexplainable
All rush across her face

She tightens her grip on the doorknob
Wanting only to go searching
For an answer, the truth, and an explanation

She hears the howling of the wind
The crashing of the raging water
And the clanging of everything that has fallen to pieces

Her adrenaline surges
While her heart rate increases
She has no idea what to do
All she wants is
For everything to become clear

Her courage and strength kicks in
She opens the door
Saying a prayer

Suddenly

The storm stops
The sun begins to peak from the clouds
Everything, thoughts and emotions
Recessed back into the boundless blue

She can't believe her eyes
The unthinkable happens
She has just weathered the storm

Impossible

She gathers everything together
Sweetly smiling
As she steps outside
Only to find a new light

Time to pick up the pieces
Take a few chances
Just by being herself
Living life and listening to her heart

Simply staying on the right road
Unafraid to weather the challenges
Of hurricane fire and ice

Second Chances

Has there ever been a time in your life
Where you feel that you've
Really made a huge mistake
Or you might have said something out of line?

Although you may not be able
To understand the effects of the situation
And all you can do is constantly sit in bewilderment
Deep down in your heart
You are secretly praying for a second chance

To many
A second chance is something
That doesn't cross the mind
Often one might feel
It's just simply too late for that next chance
And just leave things the way that they happened

This thought can often lead to a world
Of "what if" and regret
But if one is willing to have a change of heart
And give a second chance
Life can be seen in a different light

If one ponders the thought
Of giving a person a second chance
It's a very beautiful one
You can see that life is too short
To hold any regrets

We are all human
And we make mistakes
Or might just say what is in our hearts

We're not perfect
But deep down
Everyone has a good heart
And is a good person

So you see
Everyone does deserve that second chance
Though it may be fear keeping you
From granting it
Consider this

Life is too short
We may never know if
We might not wake tomorrow
We shouldn't live our lives in regret

As my momma always says
An eye for an eye
A tooth for a tooth
Just never be afraid to forgive
And harden not your heart!

What Eyes Can Reveal

The depths of one's
Very own heart and soul
Lies within
The person's piercing pupils
Also, it's been known that
One's eyes can do the talking
When one is too shy
Or afraid to speak at all
They speak what
You're truly feeling
It's almost intriguing
What one can
Observe and gain
By just gazing
Into someone's eyes
Those eyes can simply
Reveal how one
Feels about the person
Or just show their interests
The most amazing part
Is that when
You look
Straight in the eyes
Of the "one"
Instantly
There's that unique connection created
And all your uncertainties
Are surely comforted
By what the eyes
Can *truly* reveal!

Chapter 9

Crazy Little Thing Called a Man

Every woman needs one man in her life who is strong and responsible. Given this security, she can proceed to do what she really wants to do—fall in love with men who are weak and irresponsible.

—Richard J. Needham

Men! We all meet those men who drive us crazy or make us go insane. We meet those men we fall head over heels for, and they turn our lives upside down. We all have those men whom we feel we need and whom we believe need us.

Mystery of an Honest Man

I'm constantly walking around
This small but busy island
Wondering what
It would be like
To meet someone
I can put all my trust in
And be able to always be myself with
So that in return
He'll be able to
Trust me and befriend me
Building up the courage
To be a man of honesty
Speaking from his good and honest heart
Able to tell me
If I can secretly
Develop a crush on him
And to help him solve his mystery
Instead of breaking my heart
By not being honest
And finding out
That I can never help him
Solve his little mystery
Because doing so
Would only reveal
That he never told me
He had someone else
And unfortunately, for him
He'll never know
The clue to solving his mystery
Was right under his nose
All this time!

The First Guy Ever

I sit in class doing nothing
So I pull out something to work on
I'm so distracted
I can't understand why
I'm so distracted
I'm in a state of mind where
I can't eat
I can't sleep
And I always have butterflies in my stomach
Ever since I wrote him that letter
I now always have him on my mind
I recall the memories
I have of him
I deeply wish I had more
All I can think
Is how the next three months
Are going to be
Extremely long and dreadful
I long to see him
See his sweet face
Hear his soft voice
I feel I could go on forever
I wish I could communicate
With him more than
Through letters
Or over the phone
Why must this be so hard?
I hate living where I do
I live almost 1,240 miles
And nineteen hours
Away from him
You see, he's not like all the others
He's sweet

He's caring
He's compassionate
I don't care if he's not the sharpest tool in the shed
As some people call him
All I truly care about
Is his personality
You must understand
Most of the guys I meet
I tend to scare away
But not this one
At first
I have to admit
I was shocked to hear
How he feels
All my assumptions were wrong
He's the first guy to ever
And I mean ever
Call me beautiful
You ask why I like this guy so
This guy is a keeper
This guy is the first guy ever

I Hate What You Do to Me

I hate what you do to me
You turn me into
A little schoolgirl
With a secret crush

I find myself challenged
At a loss for words
Very giddy and nervous
Yet happy, speechless, and starstruck

You know how to push my buttons
Make me frustrated and confused
But make me feel
I am beautiful
You show me you care
And in this imperfect world
There's no need for impressions or perfection

You accept me for who I am
Don't have high expectations
Nor place me on a pedestal

I feel like I can tell you almost anything
You're extremely understanding
And I couldn't ask God for a better friend

You know how to make me
Laugh, smile, and enjoy life
(Never once have you made me cry)
You help me on my spiritual path
Allowing me to stay focused on the faith
Never misdirecting me
But there's just one problem

Even when I want you to leave
Or I want to walk out on you
You still remain

No matter how hard I've tried
To kick you out of my life
Because I am nothing but
A stubborn songbird
Flying this earth
With a healing heart
Far from perfect
Battered and scorned

You seem to see past it
When you look into my baby blues
Not allowing it to cause your
Boundless, beautiful dark eyes
To look the other way

I find myself
Wanting to scream at you
"For months I've been trying to tell you
How I really feel about you"
But what's the stupid point
I am most certain you've already
Fallen for someone else
Who probably fits into your world
Better than I ever could
I am only a simple Southern girl

Did I forget to mention to you
That you could have any woman you wanted
And I am sure in a million years
I could never be her
Let me tell you I am not
Afraid of being rejected
I am really used to
Men never returning the same feelings

I never really wanted
To tell you the truth
Because our friendship isn't worth
Completely jeopardizing

Besides, let's face it
I am twenty-two years old
And I've never been kissed
Nor have I had a relationship
Soon enough I'll be out of here
Beginning the next chapter of my life
We'll just have technology for communication
And I'll be focusing constantly on what's driven me
My passions, faith, and education

Just go ahead and tell me
What I think you're going to tell me
The lame response everyone else tells me
I'm so used to it
It should be overrated
Yet that's why I've refused
To open up and tell you
I have had feelings for you for a while

Even though I can't ever tell you this
To your sweet and charming face
Just know this
Your friendship to me
Is more of a treasure
Given to me from God
Than my feelings for you.

All Bottled Up

It's not easy being me
At this current time
Constantly fighting these emotions
That I've kept bottled up inside
For such a long time
Never been able to
Come out and speak
What's been on my mind
Always afraid of what you might say
Or how you might
React to the truth this time
I most certainly do not want
To jeopardize anything for either of us
There's a part of me that
Fears everything would
Change for you in a few unimaginable ways
So to keep things from
Becoming more chaotic
I decided to
Simply walk out on you
Not even to notice
What I did to you
All I intended to do was
Just surround myself
In my sport and my life
To push aside our friendship
That has touched our lives
In a magical way
And to walk out on
Someone that from our very first meeting
I knew I never wanted to
Push out of my life or
Walk away from and out on

Only for the sake of trying to
Not ruin anything or for anyone to get hurt
However, all I did was
To allow hurt to appear
In your soft and sweet eyes
And to have your heart and mind
Enter a whirlwind of confusion
Never to realize that
My own fears, doubts, and truest feelings
And drowning them out through
My unexplained actions would distill
That upon you
Mostly to be afraid to talk
With you about everything
I have been bottling up
And to admit to you
What my heart truly wants to tell you
All I really want to do is
For us to be able sit down
And talk about what is truly in our hearts

I'm Not Going Anywhere

You talk about how unsure you are
That the words I tell you are true
But you can only
Think that what I tell you is true
You say you've heard
My words from others before
And yet they've turned and walked away
Their words never seem to follow through
You're unsure if
I'm going to follow through on my words
If what I say will actually mean anything
And will actually take place
How can I show you
That I'm not going anywhere
I'm here to stay
There's no doubt in my mind
That I'm ever going to
Walk away or leave you
I know your story
And you know mine
I'm not like anyone else
For you yourself said I was different
Than the others
Those other girls
Are not me
When I looked into
Those boundless, crystallizing
Beautiful, bold eyes of yours
Truly for the first time last night
I got completely lost in them
I knew from that moment
You were the first man ever

That with every word I said
Each word came straight from the heart
I meant every word
And each word is my guarantee to you
That no matter how horrible things get
At the end of the day
I'll always be here for you
To rescue you from all that misery and pain
I'm not going anywhere
For when I look at you
I can feel it in my heart
That this friendship we have and share
Is so strong, true, and pure
More than any love I have *ever* had
Giving me your trust and heart
When you opened up to me
I knew for the first time ever
I could truly give anyone my heart, soul, and trust
Yet you were able to unlock my book's lock
You were able to understand and see the real me
You didn't run
You stayed and are still here
So you see
No matter what
At the end of the day
I could never let you go
Turn my back or run away from you
You've stuck by my side
And I've stayed by yours
I don't know how I can
Reassure you, show you, or prove to you
That I won't be like the others
Only through my actions and time will tell
But the last thing
I can tell you is
I have seen friends and men come and go
If I were to ever let you go

It would be the *biggest* mistake
And my *deepest* regret
Which I would hold with me for all eternity
I knew you coming into my life
Was the best thing
To ever happen to me.

The Man I Once Knew

I once met a man
Who had a soft touch
Loving arms, a kind and caring heart
He had the most calming and gentle voice
Of any man I have ever met
With just one gaze
Into those chestnut-brown eyes of his
You could see into his soul
Someone strong, brave, admirable, respectable
And most of all, trustworthy
A man you could befriend and know
He'd never harm you or break your heart
Only protect you and care about you
As time progressed
This man would grow on your heart
All his qualities you'd adore
You'd love the way the two of you bonded
And you'd know he'd never hurt you or
Break your heart in any fashion
Only to one day hope
To find another man who
Shared his qualities
And shared his open-mindedness
One you could be open and honest with
However, the seasons changed
The two of you went your separate ways
Then one day you came out
Told him the truth
Next thing you know
The man you once were
The best of friends with
Acted towards you in a very juvenile manner
He no longer could look you in the eyes

All he could do was act as if
You two were never friends at all
Who knew the truth would cause
Him to say, "You live and learn"
And you to say, "All good things must come to an end"
For the last time
When you gazed into
The chestnut eyes of this man
You once thought you knew
All you could see staring back at you
Was a juvenile boy who didn't
Know exactly what he wanted
Nor how to deal with the truth
Of the situation
Trapped in a twenty-two-year-old's body
For you can take the boy out of his lifestyle
But you can't take his lifestyle and ways out of him!

He Sent Me into a Trance

His eyes sent me into a trance
A feeling like none other
As I gazed into his glistening, glittering
Gorgeous green eyes
All I could do was find myself
Sent completely into an unrecognizable state of mind
No matter how much I wanted to
Say a silly phrase or a comeback
The words that I spoke openly
Were the words from my heart
Scary, I know
But this state is only explainable by God
I am not always certain of things
Yet as I found myself utterly moved
In a very divine movement
There sat a man
Of very angelic stature
A very inspiring, open-minded man
A man with a sweet Southern smile
A personality that was so genuine, unique
Honest, and graciously unforgettable
With a touch unlike any other
Soft, sensual, gentle
One that you'd never forget
(I know I cannot ever)
One that at that moment
All your fears have been shocked away
And all you can do is smile
For just one moment
I found myself
Unable to speak, only smile
And in a heavenly, true trance

The Perfect Man—A List that No Longer Exists!

For so long, I had a list, a list describing the perfect man and all the qualities he had to have. You know, ironically, I believe a part of me met the perfect man who knocked me off my feet and completely captivated my heart.

Here's the list I once had. I know every girl has a wish, has a dream. However, we always tend to find ourselves placing these forts around our hearts. So once upon a dream, I wrote this. Only simply as a meager wish and to warn you that I know he doesn't exist. Yet as a wise woman once told me, "Be careful what you wish for."

So read about the "perfect man."

I'd love to meet the perfect man. Though to be honest, I'm not really looking for him. I didn't go to college for that! Sounds corny, I know, but it's true. If he happens to read this, he knows who he is because he's already said it! (Or maybe I was just dreaming.)

The Perfect Man

He is a man with a good heart, who loves God, and family plays a key role in his life. He's a person who doesn't care if I have a little extra baggage; he just sees the good-hearted and energetic person I am. He is caring, understanding, supportive, and open-minded. He can see the goodness in everyone and is willing to lend a helping hand or a shoulder to cry on. He is respectful and thoughtful. He knows what he wants to do with his life. He knows things about me and remembers them and can read what's on my mind. When it comes to my family, he is willing to meet the parents first and get to know them and the family. And he doesn't mind my daddy's "twenty-one questions."

He enjoys spending quality time with me, even if it's discussing books, movies, TV, or anything as we walk along the shoreline and the sun sets or just sit outside underneath the South Texas stars. Or my favorite thing—just sitting together in each other's company, enjoying every moment together.

As for his looks, he'll have the most exquisite emerald eyes or he'll have those bold, boundless, and blissful blue eyes. With just a look into them, you'll see your eyes in them, and they'll glisten back at you while you see the depths of his soul. He'll have that shaggy, short brown hair that if given the opportunity, you'd run fingers through it . . . or that beach-boy blond hair.

Mostly about this man—he's confident, content, positive, and my biggest cheerleader, as I am his. He's a one-woman man. He sees me for the real Southern girl that I am and remembers what makes me so intriguing, and I see him for who he really is and how intriguing he is.

Who knows—he could even drive a Chevy or Ford truck, perfect for those drives to the middle of nowhere or for lying in the bed to enjoy the Texas stars!

Here's the thing. I wrote this very detailed list on June 20, 2006, the very day my godbrother was sent off to basic training. Yet now, as I look back, I am not even sure if the perfect man truly does exist. Maybe I was blinded by things.

None of this matters anymore. All that matters to me, if I had a list, would be—of course family and education is a given—that he would be a man of God, could manage money well, would be willing to actually sit through a Catholic service, and would love me for who I am without expecting me to change. Crazy part is, it took me finding the perfect man and getting my heart broken to see that I'm not ready for a relationship. Funny part is, the "perfect man" knows I have a list, but he doesn't even know what's in it! Life does have its twists!

Being at Peace with the King

That night, looking at the moon
She was finally able to have the courage and strength
To allow herself to face reality and generate the words
She'd been longing to say to the King for so long
Words that may appear to be soothing
But more so the truth straight from her heart

She could never believe
In a thousand years
She'd find herself staring at the man
Who caused her to tape her heart back together
Who drove her nuts
Yet at the same time
Someone she prayed would be in her life
For as long as God would allow
Gazing into those light eyes
In the room bleak as could be
She was a little in disbelief
Still, she knew this was a part of God's plan
This meeting was unexpected
But all she could do was forget
Forget about the pain he caused her

All she wanted to do
Was tell him that
She wasn't angry with him
She didn't want him to be harmed
She did want him to feel her pain
To the extent that his heart
Could be turned
Turned from being cold as ice
To warm as the bright Texas sun

This was finally her chance
To be open with him
To give her demands
To ultimately bring satisfaction
A part of her wanted to hold it in
But she knew it was the only way to let him know
Exactly what her heart had been saying

Before she knew it
Holding his attention
She felt someone had taken the key
Placed it in the box
Only opening it up to the allow the escape of the truth
This was unexpected
Yet a blessing

Observing his body language
Seeing how his smile brought life to the room
Made her realize
The man she once knew
Could possibly still exist
Not the King he had appeared to be

This was her big moment
Unashamed and unafraid
She finally could tell her truest feelings
No holding back
She told him what broke her heart
How she felt because of him
What it had been like putting her life back together

Yes, she did admit to falling for him
Though she understood
He had a purpose for being in her life
He opened her eyes
Turning her pale blues
To bright blues full of stars

It all made sense
She had been able to tell him
She could forgive him but not forget him
She held no regrets of their friendship
No regrets of time spent together
How he changed her life

There he sat
Still and motionless in his chair
Gazing her in the eyes
Seeing her emotions and feelings
Become reality
All while holding her explanation

Finally
She was at peace with herself
No longer feeling like the pauper
The society had dictated
Finally, the King no longer appeared
To be a man of invincibility in her life
Finally, she was free of him
Able to let go
With a sound mind and healed heart

The Things You Do

Your soothing voice
Your crisp whisper
Your unexplainable touch
That causes me to tremble
The warmth of your hugs
Always have a way of
Moving my body
Not to mention
Those soft, dark, mysterious eyes of yours
That have me longing to know
You and your story

As for your sweet smile
Through your radiance
You have a way of completely melting my frozen heart
I can't even remember
The last time a man
Has been able to melt my heart
And move me so much

Each time our eyes meet
My body becomes paralyzed
Your voice always
Causes me to turn my head
And the glow of your face
Stops me in my tracks
The things you do
Cannot be explained
It's all poetic and angelic
The only thing
My soul secretly
Longs to feel from you
Is your soft lips

Gently caressing my skin
Would your kiss
Be soft and sweet like you
Or cool and fiery like your outer shell
Against my flesh
Causing my body to become extremely
Weak and ungrounded

All the things you do
Are indescribable and wickedly moving
Like no other
You always catch me completely off guard
And leave me wanting more
Of that thing you do

Even if Our Worlds Never Meet

I don't even know where to begin
It seems like you and I
Are from two different worlds
And completely different lives
No doubt we've learned
To accept each other
For who we are
But at times
It seems to appear
I don't belong
Nor fit in with your lifestyle
The entourage that
You always have escorting you
Seems to fit perfectly
Into your puzzle of life

I know I asked for space and try to be open and honest
But it seems we're growing apart
I know I am different
In more ways than one
You've always accepted me
For the person I am
Yet here, lately
I am so unsure
Maybe you're secretly
Respecting my wishes
Not that I don't appreciate
What you're doing
I just never wanted it to be
The way it's turned out thus far
Yet who am I kidding
Our worlds are different
Maybe all of this

Is our wake-up call
To understand and see
Our lives are moving
In different directions
And even if we wanted
To have our worlds collide
Only a higher power
Could make it happen
Regardless of things
We never walk alone
Even if our worlds
Never meet in this lifetime

The Fiery, Mysterious, Angelic Man

He's poetic and angelic
He's cool, fiery, wickedly mysterious
He has a way with words
Extremely capable of
Sending anyone into a trance
Leaving you completely speechless
At a loss for words

He has a way of
Lighting up the room
With his causal, confident walk
And a radiant smile
Just one glance
From his mysterious, boundless
Dark, handsome eyes
Your heels are cooled
And you stop in your tracks
Completely motionless

While he approaches you
Your heart suddenly stops
Your body freezes and tenses up
Your lips stay pressed together
Your mind buzzes
Thinking what you'll say to him
In a short instance
He is near you

His touch, soft and cool
Embraces your warm flesh
Pulling you in for a hug
His strong arm
Wraps around your waist

Completely warming
Your frozen body and soul is melting

Suddenly you find you
Can't think, speak, or breathe
Only to hear
The rapid beat of his heart singing
Your eyes
Gazing into his
Mysterious, dark eyes
Seeing your eyes staring
Back into your light eyes

In that moment
You realize
That's where you could be
Forever and always

Forever and always
In the presence
And in the arms of
A poetic, cool, dark
Fiery, and mysterious
Angelic man

Conversations for Another Time

How can I say it to you
I'm scared and afraid
I've been searching for a way to run away from you
To revert back to the ways of education, faith, and sport
To avoid the idea of our paths never crossing
To never have to face you again
To admit to you this

You drive me crazy
Sometimes when I think I've got it all figured out
I've tried to figure you out
I've tried to crack the code
I tried to turn you into a piece of my work
Because I didn't know anything else
Yet deep down with you
I failed to see the truth
Since I apparently think too much

Maybe it took me getting hit by a ton of bricks
Or attempting to see the darkness turn to light
But I finally see through the broken pieces
As they come together
To make a beautiful piece of God's art
To see that little things can matter
To understand how simple kindness
Is powerful and meaningful

For so long I let the world
Try to control the way
I should be swayed
Instead of listening to my heart
And hearing what God was telling me
A part of me did it because of my pride

A part of me did it because I felt
I needed to protect things
Who was I kidding?

So here's what I realized and know
You can drive me crazy
And I believe I'm starting to know your story
I can't wait to hear more
I know you've been placed in my life for a reason
And I wouldn't have it any other way
It took me a while to see
There's so much more than what meets the eye
I'm enjoying every moment of it
And I'm thankful and feel so blessed
For all your understanding and patience
Slowly, I'm learning to understand another
Something I never believed possible
After what I've had to overcome

Hopefully, you can understand
This is all new to me
I've never truthfully felt like this before
Nor had the capability of feeling this open and free
I don't feel that I have to be in the spotlight
Nor do I have to expose everything to the world
I'm just enjoying flying by the seat of my pants
With the chance to be free, open, and me
Enjoying our random encounters
The world being clueless
Just God guiding us

I know I've made mistakes
I know I'm not perfect
But I am a daughter of Christ
Maybe you can see the light, too
And the changes that occur when
You're willing to break the chains

Not even worrying about labels
I've even thrown out my list of perfection

I'm not sure what's going to happen
But maybe you wouldn't mind
Walking into the light with me
Just shooting the breeze
Seeing how we're characters in each other's stories
We'll continue to appreciate each other
And see where we're meant to be
Unafraid, unashamed, seeing that we're wonderfully made
No worries about the past
Only seeing what miracles that God has planned

So what do you say
Do we have some conversations for another time?

Someone Else's Prince Charming

Every girl dreams of her Prince Charming
Finding her and taking her away
From the craziness of the world
And helping her live her happily ever after
Allowing their imperfect world
To be absolutely perfect
Yet who are we kidding?
Is there such a thing as
"Happily ever after"
Does Prince Charming exist?
Will he ever come and find his princess?

What if in our heart and gut
Our Prince Charming does exist
But the man who waltzes in comes
In the least likely fashion

At first you absolutely despise him
Can't believe a man like him
Has been paired up with you
Then suddenly you realize
The description of your perfect yet imperfect man
In the most peculiar of ways
You seem to be living your fairy tale
Every girl dreams about (in some way)

Eventually, it's shattered when you find out
He's already someone else's Prince Charming
So why wish for a happily ever after
When your Prince Charming
Always turns out to be another princess's Charming
Riding off into the sunset
Along the seashore of ever, ever after

Afraid to Face Him

She admires his works and gifts from afar
She knows he has been blessed with a natural ability
She can see him and his work going very far
Secretly, how can she tell him
"If I ever need anything done, personally, I would love to use you"?

Some may argue with her
Call her logic a bunch of nonsense
But in her mind
She believes she'll never feel worthy
Of his talents, work, and worth
Granted, she would love to be captivated
By anyone's work
Letting her beauty, grace, and poise shine
Yet she feels she's nothing like his other muses
She can't ever tell him
She can just go on wishing and dreaming

She knows this is the man she can confide in
The man who knows about her ghosts
The man she can blow up on
She's heard his story, too
And seen him be himself, as well
This isn't abnormal for friends
He isn't a man she is afraid of
This was a man she trusts
And realizes God has placed in her life for a reason
Still, there is some hesitation

Even if she deep down
Knows how beautiful God had created her
The beauty she sees every time
She recognizes her reflection

Or sees a photograph of herself
It makes her smile and thank God
Feeling or believing she'd be just as good
As his previous muses had
Still keeps crossing her mind

You know something funny?
She is just a small-town girl
With no real sense of fashion
Can't really get herself all dolled up
Without the help of another
Yet deep down loves getting all dolled up
Being able to soak up the moment
Letting the camera capture it all
I guess you could say
She's like every other girl

For some reason this man
Baffles her in so many ways
As much as she would like to work for him
She can't because of her own fears
She may be confident
She may be able to handle doing things independently
She's faced many things and won or overcome them
But to face him
Would be like shattering the lens

Up the Fairy Tales

When we're little girls
Our mothers read us the stories of girls
Having their happily ever after
Finding their Prince Charming
And the world they live in
Makes complete sense
Yet they failed to mention
When we got older
We'd have to understand that the truth is
Reality doesn't always allow for those fairy tales to take place
Reality suggests fairy tales are just a misconception
Maybe if when we were younger
Someone would have told us
Happy endings could occur
However, we have to understand
Reality would bring moments in time
Of doubt, disappointment, tears, fears
Heartaches, and more
We'd be more patient and willing
To adjust to the curveballs life
Would bring us
Now, we're living in a day and age
We have to deal with aggregation
And not understanding why the man
We supposedly love or is in love with us
Causes us to cry and want to give up on love
Or my favorite one
When a boy teases you
It really doesn't mean he likes you
Unless we have someone who's brave enough
To challenge the misconceptions of life
We discover when we fall apart
WE FALL APART

Praying someone will pick up the pieces
And help us come back down to earth
If we ever allow ourselves to feel
That man will have to deal with the wrath
The first man caused
Now needless to say
As the times change
We must change
Promising ourselves to stay strong
Stand our ground
And fall in love with a higher power
Thus never giving up hope and faith
If we were to remember
It was written long before we were created
"Love is patient, love is kind"
Suggesting to us
That in the good times and the bad
We can stay strong and see
Positive outcomes only
My philosophy is this
Life is not always going to be a real-life fairy tale
And Prince Charming may not always come to you
In the time when you want him to rescue you
However, stay focused
Don't be scared and just live life
Never let anyone keep you from
Achieving the goals you long desired
Then it's all going to be great
Or as a friend of mine once said
Fairy tales are just a bunch of made-up garbage
So that every girl can always be looking for love
Living life and ignoring the truth of it
Because life really isn't a fairy tale
It's just something to mess us up
I say, forget fairy tales
Forget finding Prince Charming
And don't ever think that you need a man
To help you live your life

Just always trust in the Lord
And say your prayers daily
So here's what I say
Up the fairy tales!

Does Charming Really Exist?

Nearly half a decade ago
On a hot summer night she'd never forget
She took out pen and paper
And began writing out a description of a man
A man whom she'd considered to be
Her ideal, perfect man
A simple man
Who would probably never exist
Thus she'd never have to worry about
Dealing with the pain and disasters of a broken heart
Never in a million years
Would she find herself
Reflecting on the qualities of this man
She created so long ago
Yet funnily enough, over a great meal
On her twenty-third birthday
The reflection did occur
Without even having any idea
It seemed the description of this man
Was about a man
She would have never considered
A man who had a great lifelike
Almost unpredictably surprising quality
The qualities of the man
The joyful women were describing
Seemed to match up perfectly
With the man she described long ago
The craziest part of it all
Is even though the man they were talking about
Didn't meet every quality of her ideal, perfect man
The man they were describing seemed to be
Created in the image that God
Had wanted this girl to see

The image that aligned so perfectly
With the description of a man
She only dreamed about
Sadly, she found herself praying
Praying to God that this Charming
She had once created
On that warm and still summer night
Would actually exist to her one day
As she sat there
Mentally reflecting on this man
Listening to the ladies
Talk about this man
Whom she could always tell
Was a man with a beautiful soul
And a God-loving heart
Through his sweet embrace
Angelic smile
Trembling touch
She was able to sense this man
Would never hurt a soul
Would always lead by faith
Be led to the cross
And follow his heavenly Father
Someone who could make anyone
Feel earthly secure and know with him
He's full of the spirit and able to lead
The followers out of harm's way
Who was she kidding?
Was it earthly possible
Her perfect man she created long ago
Would actually be at her doorsteps finally?
Does Charming really exist?

Draw the Line

Where do I draw the line
Realize that this dream
Of you and I
Finding ourselves meeting again
Is only a figment
Of my big, bold imagination?
It seems every time
We mention meeting
There's no greeting one another
We always end up
Being where we're supposed to be
Living our lives
Doing what we're called to do
Why should we even conceive the notion
Of trying to catch up
After all these years
We should just continue
Going through the motions
Simply realizing we have to
Draw a line somewhere
Since we're going nowhere
And most importantly
We have to understand
God's in control
Doing what he believes is best
Leaving some things an unspoken mystery
Thus, let's wake up from the dream
Stop trying to make up for lost time
You stop saying you're sorry
For us not getting to catch up
And draw the line

Chapter 10

Loving Papa God

God loves us more in a moment than anyone could in a lifetime.

—Author Unknown

A loving relationship with God is one I have developed. My faith is constantly growing. These poems I have written are my inner thoughts on sharing my personal experiences with God and our growing relationship.

Coming Clean About the Mystery Man

Sitting in the white church
Looking at Jesus
Nailed upon the cross
I began to ask God to help me
Help to be forgiven for what I've done wrong
Help me to forgive myself for the times I have been angry
For the past three months I have held a little too much anger
Towards someone who could possibly deserve it
But I
As a daughter of Christ
Should go without anger
Something must be done

My time came to really become more open
Dig deep down inside
To rid myself of this anger and frustration
Something I thought I had gotten rid of two weeks prior
But a part of me
Still believed wasn't totally honest

I could see in my mind
Me telling this boy
Just please always be yourself
Always be honest and never hide behind anything
Yet here I was posing behind things
I was lying to him about something

How simple would it have been
To just tell him straight to his face
Look deep into his stained-glass eyes
And tell him
"Yes, my friend
You were the one who shattered my heart

Not because of the reasons you might think
But for the reasons that the world may find
Hard to even comprehend or find just cause
My reasoning is this
You slammed the door in my face
You acted as if you were two people
Started to treat me differently when people were around
Almost as if you were ashamed of me
Which is your problem
We should be accepting and loving
I've often prayed to God
Asking him where the man
Who was very full of life
God's grace and love
Has drifted off too
Not this boy who has faded
And begun to hide away
I know you've got a problem with me
And getting to travel to Sydney
So be honest about why you've started to roll your eyes
Don't lie
Also learn to follow through
If you say you're going to do something
Do it!
Friends learn to communicate with each other
Friendships are a two-way street
Learn to pick up your little phone
Check in on me and say, 'Hey, how ya doing?'
If a week goes by and there's no exchange of salutations
Regardless of it all
I'm still going to love you no matter what you've done
And always support you, even if you're not involved or
Shining as bright as a star
Because that's what friends do
I forgive you and only pray for you."

Maybe in time
The good Lord will allow me

The opportunity to come clean with him
Yet for now
God knows the truth
He knows where my heart lies
He knows where my intentions are
Hopefully it'll all become clear
And I'll soon learn the importance
Of patience and retaining grace

For now
I'll just understand
Through Christ all things are possible
And he'll one day give me the understanding
Of why everything happens
And why people are in my life

Longing for You and Wanting to Hear Your Song

She wakes from a slumber
Only to find herself in a trance.
She longed to see him again.
She longed to feel his touch
To feel the warmth of his smile
To feel the light of his eyes
Stopping her in her tracks
And to hear his sweet voice
Sing her true love's song.

As she thought of this
She was uncertain what had
Happened to her while she dreamed
Thinking of all the glorious deeds
God had done for her
And those she loved, knew, and
Would one day come into contact with
How awesome and powerful
The Heavenly Father is.

The more and more
She attempted to no longer be
In the unexplainable trance.
She couldn't escape it.

All she could say
To herself was
"God, you're mighty to save
You can move mountains
Bless us with beauty, talents, gifts
Hopes, faith, and love
And have
Created us beautifully in your image

We can never thank you enough
Just know your grace is enough
You know
I can't wait to see you face-to-face
When you've called me home
However, now I know
You're with me
Because I'm never walking alone
And you always place people in my life
I need to come into contact with."

No sooner had she shouted these words
She got up, smiled, and said
"Good morning, God, thank you for letting me
Long for you and hear your song."

When I Think of You

When I think of you
There are no questions to be asked
You're my lover and my best friend
You're my defender of the night
You know exactly what to say
You make me completely speechless
When you wrap your arms around me
I feel nothing but your heavenly powers
It's like my heart is on fire
And I don't want it to be put out

When I think of you
There's no one else I'd rather be with
I know when I'm with you
I am home and free from danger
The angels are singing their song of praise
Our mother and father could not be happier
Nothing could explain my feelings

When I think of you
I think how I'm your princess
And you're my prince
We're the happiest couple
Dancing the dance of life
Seeing how beauty comes from the heart

When I think of you
I think how close we've become
How much I have the desire
To be your servant and be yours
I only want to strive to the best of my abilities

When I think of you
I have peace of mind
I don't want to ever leave your side
I see how amazing you are
How loving you are
And how I only pray
You'll send me a companion
Who has the same feelings towards you as me
When I think of you
I know you are my King

What Our Father Does for Love: The Lessons He Teaches Us

We often meet people who come into our lives
Teach us some amazing lesson
Often one you'll never forget
It can be seen as
A blessing from our Heavenly Father
The sad part
Which we can sometimes not see
Is that the person or people who
Teach us their lessons
Don't always stay forever
Many times people come in and out of our lives
Like a revolving door
Touching our hearts
And leaving their imprint on it
Yes, it may hurt
Knowing that you'll never
Either speak to them or see them again
But their lessons and memories will
Be a part of you forever
God blesses us with the power
Of having the gift of memory
And that's something
No one, not even a demonic source
Can take away
We just pray to our Father
And thank him for everything
Realizing what he's doing is out of love

Chapter 11

Hopeless Romantic

I am a bit of a hopeless romantic. I really do have a faith and a belief in love, and when I love, I love hard.

—Melanie Fiona

"Hopeless romantic" is a phrase that could be used to best describe me. I have faith and hope in falling in love and relationships. When I fall, I do fall hard. The poems I have written for this chapter can only emphasize how much I am a hopeless romantic.

Hopeless Romantic

For as long as I can remember
I have been a young woman
Who always speaks of
Love and romance as something
So mystical and magical
A sweet symphony of
Fantasy and delight
Something so beautiful
Inexplicable, unexplainable

Yet in reality
I am a hopeless romantic
Who has dreamed about
Meeting the "perfect man"
And knowing what it is
To truly feel true love again

I am a hopeless romantic
Who has only been in
One long relationship
That was solely long distance
And sadly ended
As the spring of 2005 appeared

I am a hopeless romantic
Since the loss of
The man I once loved
I use my experience of
True love and romance
To inspire and encourage others
To never give up on love

I am a hopeless romantic
Who believes everyone
Should have their romantic wishes
Truly fulfilled and completed
And to be able to find
True bliss and happiness

I am a hopeless romantic
Who has always lived her life
Hidden away from the world
Living and breathing her
Life passions and work
And never giving up
On her dreams and saving the "world"

I am a hopeless romantic
Who dreams of becoming
A woman of distinction
Impacting the lives she touches
Only to save music education
By speaking for those who can't
And truly making a difference

I am a hopeless romantic
Who has had her heart broken
And is afraid of learning to love again
Afraid of putting her trust in another man
To only end up completely heartbroken

I am a hopeless romantic
Who is full of life
Learning each day
Living each day to the fullest
Savoring each moment
Being an independent woman

But I am also a hopeless romantic
Who has discovered that

For so long I have
Had this wall built up
Avoiding the desire for love and romance

Somehow I have seen that
Deep down I long
To know what it's like
To be in love and in a relationship
I dream of actually knowing what it
Feels like to have the "perfect man"
In my life
By my side, seeing the best in me
Supporting me as I support him

I am a hopeless romantic
Who has dreams and goals
Who mostly just wants to share
The love and kindness the Heavenly Father has given her

Can't Wait to Meet Him

I'm only human
I have feelings and emotions
That can become overwhelming
A heart that's been
Turned cold and broken
Yet slowly healing
And full of love
I'm tired of being part
Of the jars of hearts collected
By those who have stabbed it
I just can't take it anymore
I want fireworks exploding
Letting the joys of life
Ignite the night sky
Sharing the moment with you
I'm a woman of faith
Opening her heart
To all of God's plan
I know I could wait one thousand years for you
To see my character and know
God has called us to be together
Taking two broken souls
And creating the perfect circle
I know you're the one
Who makes me a better person
By inspiring me daily
Because of your strength and love for God
With you I can be me
Like a giddy child
I know magic is always there
All the wait was worth it
And I'm blessed he's
Called us to live out our lives

For him
I know we're two people
Who are there
Full of love
At our best and our worst
Through faith, hope, and love
Everything makes sense
Even when the whole world
Doesn't understand
We'll feel the fire
Of a beautiful friendship
And know
We are each other's best friend
Realizing God planned this
Until then
I'll pray for you
And tell God
Some things in life are worth waiting for
Or should I say, melt for
Wherever you are
Whoever you are
I'll wait for you
Knowing my ghosts are gone
And my heart is ready to
Be shared
Even though I'm only human
With you I could never crash
I end by saying
I can't wait to meet you one day

What is Love?

Throughout our lives
We are constantly pondering the thought
Of one of the greatest gifts
That God has blessed us with

However, it seems half the time
We are constantly unsure of what it is
We question ourselves
About the essences of it
About how it truly belongs
To the realm of the unseen
We have the longing
And the desire to know
What it truly feels like

The gift that I speak of
Is the four letter word: L-O-V-E

The biggest question that
Is asked today amongst
Not only ourselves
But our family, friends, and coworkers
Is "What is love?"

After hearing this question daily
As well as pondering the thought
I've chosen to express my belief
Of what love really is

Love is the greatest gift that God can bless anyone with
Love is something so powerful and magical
That it cannot be explained

Love is the feeling that you could be anywhere or do anything
And you know that you can make it through
The hardest of times because of it

Love is something that cannot be questioned
When you know you are in love
You have this feeling of invincibility
No matter what anyone says
Because of love
Nothing can knock you down
And you know at the end of the day
You've always got something to live for and smile about

True love is the one gift and feeling
That you know from the moment you
Look into that person's eyes or you meet them
That it exists
It is real, pure, and perfect in its own way
You know in your heart
It can last forever

Love is the feeling that
Makes your heart sing
Butterflies appear in your stomach
Brings a smile that shines as bright as the South Texas sun
Not to mention
It gives you the belief that everything feels so right
When you and your other half are together

However, if you are ever apart
You know you can look up at the stars in the sky
And know that love is looking at the same sky
You can be miles apart
And nothing can divide your love

Lastly, love is
The feeling that your world is fully complete
The idea no one is higher than God

But he has blessed you with the greatest gift
And someone so special in your life
Who is your best friend and lifelong teammate
And will be with you from beginning to end
As you will for them

Call love crazy or whatever you want to
Call love a joke
I don't rightly care
However, when it appears in your life
You'll know
Heart, mind, body, and soul

Just whatever you do
Never be afraid to
Experience the greatest gift
If you have a broken or blackened heart
Never be afraid of taking a second chance
To deny the heart to feel love
Is like denying oneself life
Always remember
God blesses us with
Three wonderful gifts
Faith, hope, and love
But the greatest gift is love
And remember
True love always waits

Love Is Like Life

To feel that first kiss, only to suddenly wake up and find the universe tilting and grasping in front of my eyes. So many things are happening for the first time, many new ones. The world is opening and closing at the same time. To taste that first kiss, to feel the first ecstasy of love. To have this illusion that these feelings will happen again and again.

Do you know that
I am happy with you
To be here with you
I am alive
I feel as if
I've felt heaven
Simply to know
An hour of eternity
A moment in your eyes
Losing myself
Being able to see
My eyes staring back at me
And seeing the depths of your soul

Love is like life
Merely longer
Love is like death
During the grave
Love is
The fellow of the Resurrection
Scooping up the dust and
Chanting "Live!"

Falling in Fall

I couldn't help
But have to hold back
My true emotions.
When our eyes met
You smiled with sweet delight.
At that moment
My heart was racing
My arms weak and trembling
From wanting to hug you
The first moment I saw you.
And the little voice inside my head
Screaming what I really wanted to say to you
"Thank God you're back.
I've really missed you!
A part of me thought
You had run off with a Vegas girl
And weren't coming back."
However, I avoided my heart and mind
For if I did speak the truth
You'd know that somehow
Between our exchange of smiles
Through our conversations
And summer turning into fall
I had found myself
Falling for you!

Hope You'll Find Me on the Dance Floor

Words can't often explain
The actions and emotions I am portraying
When your presence is made

Every time we talk
Life beings to dance
And we're both spinning
On the dance floor of life

While on the floor
I hear the song
That the band is playing
The singer is simply singing
The song that my soul's
Been longing to perform

The singer begins
Singing these unexplainable words

"Every time we meet
I wanna live in that
Sweet moment forever
But let's face reality
You and I know we're not
From the same walks of life

"In a heartbeat you'd have
All the ladies wooed with
Your very poetic words and stimulating soft voice
Sending them into a deep trance
Their bodies instantly frozen in place
They become speechless
Unable to breathe or think

Just longing to see what this 'angel' will do next
Only waiting for you
To choose your beautiful princess."

The band continues to accompany
The singer on stage
Yet somewhere in the midst
We hear the singer sing these lines
After a sweet guitar solo
"Never in a million years
Will I be able to tell you, my friend
You're like my best friend
Understanding and no explanation
Is expected or needed

"You allow me to be free and me
And most of the time
We seem to compliment each other
With some of the sweetest compliments

"With you
There are no questions asked
Life just makes sense

"Most of all I just want you
To know the truth and what's in my heart
I have these unexplainable feelings for you
That have been locked away in my soul

"My soul always wants to yell
'I love you and I think I'm falling for you'
I've dreamed of telling you this
Kissing you on the cheek

"And telling you
I just needed to be honest with you
But I do know
You and I are traveling down

Two completely opposite directions
And I am sure
You've already found your Beauty

"Don't worry, I am not afraid
Of being rejected by you
You won't break my heart
For our feelings for each other
Are mostly not mutual

"It's no biggie
I am sure I would've
Eventually blurted out
I'd only hurt you in the end
It's what I do best
Or just thanks for your time
And now you know
What I've been trying to tell you."

As the singer finishes the song
The floor clears
There I am
All alone
Only to realize
This whole scene
Was only an illusion and a figment of my imagination
I could never have the guts
To tell you what's on my heart
Just to ruin a good friendship

Yet in my dancing dream
I would love to tell you
"Hopefully, one day, you'll join me on the dance floor."

Voice of an Angel

Even when my students
Have driven me up the wall
Used profanity towards me
Or I have just had a really bad day

I close my eyes
And your soft and sweet voice
Begins to sing in my head

Your voice seems to be
The peace and serenity I need
To make it through
The toughest times
It's so soothing
Sweet, innocent, and pure

How is this even possible?
I am most certainly unsure
Nor am I over thinking it all

I just know at times
It is something I pray to God
Thanking him for
Blessing you with it
And being able to share it
With me in this crazy world
We're both living in

Your voice
Is the voice of a guardian angel
Sent from heaven above
Always with me
On the unexplainable journey I'm traveling

Can I Just Have One Dance?

Can I just have one dance with you
I'd love to have us
Soak up the energy and excitement
That life presents us
I'd love to enjoy the moment
And quality time with you

I'm sure we'd strike up a good conversation
Making each other laugh and smile
Never letting our eyes disconnect
Realizing that this dance
Was simply meant for us

After the music stops
I'm sure we'd still be
Holding each other's arms
Waiting for that one perfect moment

Our eyes meet
Hands softly touch
Unexpectedly, our lips lock
Sharing a passionate true love's first kiss

Years down the line
We could surely look back
And only laugh with each other
About what happened
When you danced that
One special dance with me

Chapter 12

In Memory of Tuesday

No day but today.

—Jonathan Larson

Tuesday. A man I can never forget. He was the first man who taught me to love, live, believe, and see things from a different perspective. He was the first soul mate I ever had. Though he has left this earth, he left an imprint on my heart. As one of his favorite musicals, *Rent*, says, “No day but today.”

Hey, Tuesday: A Letter to a Dead Man

Hey, Tuesday,

It's me. I know it's been years since we've talked. Yet I know you're looking down on me from up above. I know you can see what I see between those two young jennies—so understanding, so innocent, yet so young. They are compassionate and carefree. I look at these two, and sometimes they admire you and me, baby. You know, I still remember the long conversations we used to have. Those little sweet nothings we used to share. Not to mention the things we once used to share. The crazy part of it all is we could really relate to sharing a secret, maybe forbidden love. Regardless of how we ended, all I can do is think of you and the sweet things you used to do.

Over the past few days, I've seen these two and how they're with each other. Baby, I swear that they are us and what should've been and what could've been. Seeing these two and their love for each other is the love we used to know and share. Even though we never got the chance to hold hands, look into each other's eyes, fall asleep in each other's arms, or even say "I love you" to each other face-to-face, they are showing that love. True love. The love God gave to us. Although ours was short-lived, I know it was real, and you'll forever be in my heart.

Tues, maybe it's how you always told me to live and love for today or how you preached to me about the future, not having a care about tomorrow but just for today. Ultimately, how we should live for today with no regrets. I am unsure what it is yet, what I should try to tell these two.

The times I've seen them together, it's a great photo opportunity to capture their magical love on camera. You'd probably even write a song about it and play it on your guitar. I just know the beautiful and poetic song it'd be. I am sure your portfolios of pictures would align perfectly. Much better than I could tell it or see it.

Now it's confession and time to ask my best friend and soul mate for some advice. I don't know if what I'm doing is right. They've both confided in me. They are both unsure of what tomorrow brings and what'll happen at the stroke of seven tomorrow night. I know I've been a female Hermes and the big sister, but is that enough?

Sometimes I wish I could tell them to just hold on and never give up on each other. You didn't, despite people calling us crazy and telling us long distance would be the end of us, not to mention our age difference. But, baby, we did make it, even though temptation and complication were there.

I know how we parted wasn't exactly how we planned it, yet I know my name was the last name you said. Although we had our ups and downs, the time we shared is a fairy tale in which I saw and see these two very mature and loving kids are telling the world. Just telling them our story and how we were the lucky ones lost but found. I know as I write this to you. I know what I can tell them tonight on their last night, when they'll share a "no secret, no complications" zone. I'll tell them what you used to tell me from your song for me, Escape's "I'll Be There."

Over land and over sea, just think of me and I'll be there.

When you're afraid, just close your eyes and think of me, I'll be there.

And regardless of anything, no one can most certainly tear them apart. Every time they are afraid or alone, they should just know that they hold the key to each other's hearts. Oh, and my favorite little line, "When scared or alone, think of me because I'm always thinking of you, forever and always. Just keep holding on and living, no day but today."

Tues, thanks for always listening and knowing what to say.

I'll see you soon.

Love always. Forever.

Me

She's His Beauty, Grace, and Love Divine

She's his beauty and his grace
His inspiration and hope
She's his encouragement and strength
His love's divine and holder of his key
To the lock on his heart
That has longed to be unlocked
She's his best friend and other half
His one he can run to
When he feels like there's no one else in this world
Aside from music
She *is* his world and rock
His one true companion
Through the power of the heavens above
And of all of God's grace
She's the one
He's star struck and breathless with just one look
Into her beautiful, brave, blissful baby blues
She's his eternal end
His reason to breathe and to smile
And reason to want to strive past anything and everything
No matter what temptation or stress comes into play
He knows she can be miles about or even a short distance away
Yet his heart, soul, beauty, grace, and best friend is forever his
For he can hear her call a mile away and see her sweet smile in his mind
He can hear his jennie singing their song
Waiting for the day they can sing their duet
She's his and he is hers
Heart and soul, mind and body
Their spirits are as one
So innocent, young, and so pure
Most simply knowing
She's his beauty, grace, and love's divine

There's No More Crying Here

From the first time I mentioned
I would cry when it was all over
Or when something great happened
He always told me, "Don't cry"

Every time I ever felt or feel remotely close to crying
The tears failed to fall
It seems the few times
I have cried were when
Reality started to set in
Yet I'll never tell him

Somehow, this man
Out of nowhere, let me add
Has gotten under my skin
His voice into my head
Leaving his imprint on my heart

So many times I have wanted to scream
The only times I do are in my dreams
It's like all this emotion is shut in
With nowhere to escape

Funny part of it all
Even when I want to cry
Those essential tears of joy
All I do is feel
This huge smile grow on my face
Producing that radiant glow of sunshine
My voice producing a song
One that only longs
The world to hear

How here lately
I've found where I belong

I used to cry with no hesitation
It would come naturally
But now who do I have to blame
It's lame to put the blame on him

I accepted his challenge
Realizing that for so long
I've just always wanted to cry regardless of happiness or sorrow
Nowadays when I want to cry out tears, I can't

Truth of it all is
I simply hear his voice
The image of his sweet Southern smile appears
So no more tears can I cry

This is only indicating
The journey isn't over
And great things are happening constantly
Allowing those tears to turn into songs
Spoken or written
Reminding us
There's no crying here

Chapter 13

Letters to You

To send a letter is a good way to go somewhere without moving anything but your heart.

—Phyllis Theroux

Every letter I have written in this chapter has been a letter to express my emotions and feelings to the receiver. Within each letter, there are different concerns being addressed and feelings being shared. I hope each letter comes as an interesting letter you would receive in the mail.

Dear Sir

Dear sir:

I want to take this opportunity
To tell you thank you
For all you've done for me
I know I wouldn't be
The woman or future teacher
I am today without your
Unconditional care, kindness, support, and guidance

I learned so much from you
You helped develop a passion
For the area I've been studying
For over four years
To have the courage and strength
To face the lives that
I come into contact with
And have the ability to be me

However, now it's time to tell you
Your chick has hatched
Become a strong, hopeful, and fearless songbird
From you
Your chick has learned how to fly and survive, too

I believe you should know
It's time for this songbird's wings to spread
And soar amongst the endless sky
Never forgetting who taught her
And where her home is

Also just know
As I take this flight of life

I'll never forget
All the words of wisdom
The countless hours you spent training me
And prior instruction you've given to me
Not to mention the good times we've shared

I always know when in doubt
How to handle whatever
Curveball is thrown at me
Never afraid to hit it

Now that you've done
Your call of duty
Always understand
I've learned from the best

So if you do care to find me
As I soar above you
Turn to the western sky
And there I'll be
Who knows, I might even sing a song for you
While I pass by

Please understand
This solo journey I am flying
Is my chance
To follow my calling
Never wondering what might have been
Or if I was living out someone else's dream

So I say to you
When I take that flight
I want you there
While I depart
But understanding
This is your chance
To learn to let me go
And just be delighted

I'm singing my song
Because I have you with me
And I'm unafraid to venture
Out into the unknown

As I travel the endless sky
No matter where we are
We'll always have our connection
And you are a handprint on my heart
And I know
You'll always be waiting for me
To come back home
Whenever you need me
Or to just let you know I am alive

So to you, sir
Thank you for being in my life
Fulfilling your destiny
Leaving your mark in my life
Being that trusting
Confidant and friend
Who came into my life
When I was completely lost

I couldn't have asked
For a better person
To help me
On my path of discovery
To hatch and become a songbird
Who has found her way
And is not afraid of taking this flight

Now, as I take off for my next
Destination in life
Know I'll be back some day
Hoping each of us
Are living our lives to the fullest
Full of love, prosperity, and faith

I'm sure when I come back
I'll be looking forward to meeting
The Mrs. and your chicks, especially IV
And I'll be hand-delivering to you
That New York best seller
You once inspired me to write

Regardless of where I go
Or where you go
We'll always be with each other
And I'll always know
You were the man
Who taught me how to fly

Adios,
Your spring songbird

Dear Mr. Know-It-All

Dear Mr. Know-It-All,

How are you today? I hope you're doing swell. Hopefully things in your life are falling into place perfectly and you do not have to face any adversity. Maybe the stars are in your corner and they are shining so brightly; even in the dark of night, you are able to keep on rising up the ladder of life. I hope that you are continuing to be a great leader and example to all those you represent. Isn't the world so lucky to have been blessed with a man like you?

I have a question for you, though. Sometimes I wonder if you've ever had to face adversity and overcome many odds. I wonder if you have ever had people put you down, telling you that you were not going to be successful in your sport or ever make anything of yourself. I wonder if you have ever had a day in your life that someone hasn't slandered your name or spoken negatively about you behind your back, with no one defending you and you feeling like you're all alone. I wonder if you have to live with the idea that because you're from a one-horse town, you'll never make it out of here. Most importantly, I wonder if you have ever had to face so many demons because they would not accept you for numerous reasons. Do you know what it's like to walk in an outcast's shoes? I know what I see when I look into your dark eyes, but I could be completely wrong about you.

Maybe none of my questions can be answered nor responded to; however, I hope they do bring some light into your eyes. I never meant to seem too pushy or an enforcer; I just wanted to defend myself and speak the truth, as I've been brought up. Not every person you meet will have been raised in the big-city life or around more than two thousand people. Hopefully, through these past few days, you will have an understanding of how some Southerners react differently and interpret things differently than other people. Not everyone has been influenced the same and taught the same virtues and values. Ultimately, maybe you as well as I have learned something from this experience.

Oh, how our Lord works in mysterious ways. If only I could have an understanding why our paths had to cross and our diverse differences appeared. Maybe one day you'll be able to tell me your thoughts, revealing them to us all, and my mind can be put at ease, but for now, we'll just have to go on wondering.

Anyhow, I hope this fresh start provides a great and blessed adventure. I know the good Lord's our captain and knows what he is doing. We, as children of Christ, have to appreciate each other's talents and gifts, and encourage harmony to the world, which we live in; not understanding everyone is the same, and it is our responsibility to make it right. No more misunderstanding is needed. It is not about us always being know-it-alls.

Until our paths cross again,

A not-so-typical Texan

Dear Michael

Dear Michael,

As crazy or out of place as this letter might sound, I believe in my heart it's important that I tell you what I am about to tell you. Scripture tells us we are to forgive each other as I have forgiven you. Now, I know it isn't something typically discussed amongst young adults; however, the topics of forgiveness and reconciliation are two things that do need to be addressed. Yes, I know that we came to a mutual understanding and believed we should start off on the right foot, but there's a part of me that is having a difficult time letting go of the cross fire and starting over.

You and I both know you're a blessed and great person who has a heart and spine. Deep down, from what I could see, you're gentle, humble, and earnest. You're not the person the populous crowd wants you to be. In public, you're this cool, witty superstar who just does what he can to maintain his reputation, but in private you're the complete opposite. I say this only because your actions speak louder than words. Thus, I am left baffled and petrified.

For when I see you in public and try to speak with you, I continue to still be full of anger, rage, and bewilderment. I still envision throwing the cup of ice water on you. You're no Golden Boy, and your actions need to be addressed. All I can do is seek justification and prove that your ways are not to be overlooked. Additionally, I begin to seek an answer on why you decided to target me in the first place. When I think back to what you wrote me, I was blown away and speechless. It was unexpected and humanized. I could tell that it was the real you writing me. I could tell you had a golden heart distilled with gentleness, humbleness, and warmth. Your response suggested you were not a spineless, immature Y-chromosome with a heart as cold as ice. The man who spoke to me was one worth fully forgiving and maybe one day calling a friend. However, three days later, your actions, kindly yet unspoken, suggested your heart was frozen and deeply in need of prayer. Just when I believed we had truly reconciled, I was fooled. Nevertheless, I realized I had not fully forgiven you and let go of all the negativity you caused me.

My main point after all my prologue has been spoken is to tell you I, in some odd way, understand why your actions are the way they are and realize although I may not know your story, there are not a lot of factors I haven't taken into consideration. As I begin again for me and talk with God, all I can say is I am relinquishing your power and I forgive you wholeheartedly. I no longer want to hang on and walk around with a hardened heart. I, being the selfless, honest Texas woman I am, simply wish you well. I hope one day you can be fully distilled with an ignited heart and soul, no longer adhering to the populous crowd, and always be the kindhearted good ol' boy with a gentle soul that spoke to me in that message. I hope your light will always shine.

As for me, I'll slowly but surely be able to let it all go, making my heart no longer hard. I'll be able to continue glorifying God and continue to serve him, moving one step closer to my doctorate. I know that it may take some time, but I'll be better off and have my power back. While I make my stride to let go, I'll try to bury the hatchet. I only wish you will understand why this is significant to both of us. I know it doesn't make sense, because we're practically strangers, but we have to realize God's placed us in each other's paths. Now we have to endure our Father's plan and see what it teaches us. Ultimately, I only wish you the best and hope you get what you deserve.

Anyhow, Michael, just know one thing—I forgive you.

Aloha a hui hou,
Me

Honesty

I wrote this during adoration on Friday. I thought about how Father Francis was talking about restoring relationships.

Mate,

You asked me to be honest about the football team, and as much as I wanted to let it all out, I had to resist. I believe in certain situations something like this is better left unspoken. Not everyone needs to hear it. I'm sure by now, you've figured out what I was doing. If it had been just you and me, I could have been open and told you what I am about to say. I just wish I could say it while looking into your stained-glass eyes.

Thanks in advance for being so understanding.

When I first got here, I dreamed of nothing but football twirling, football games, and the little fantasy I would catch some dashing player's eyes and it'd be like in the movies or other stories I've been told by my twirling friends, but God had other plans. Getting to compete at an international invitational competition in spring 2012 and being named sports editor allowed me to see where two of my greatest passions were: performing and sports writing. After finding out the decision we all made about competition only for the uni for my remaining time, I had to learn not to live in shame and disappoint people.

For a year I avoided games because of work, using the Internet or radio to listen. It even helped when you told me you didn't care if I was there or not. As much as I wanted to be there to show my support for you, mate, and the team, you gave me an easy way out of avoiding questions about my absence on the field. Even though my heart was broken.

Through training for competition season, I thought how awesome it would be to perform at volleyball or basketball games, but God continued to allow me to see I could respect the programs playing by not performing. While in Australia, those two months training and competing gave me a new perspective on life. Pick on my sport all ya want, but by being in the gym more, I concentrate on getting healthier, letting my body grow stronger and my technique improve to be ready for the 2017 international team trials in 2016. In the end, I can just be me, and hopefully you'll support me as I have always been supporting you.

I meant what I said the other night. I love you guys and respect you. My heart bleeds for the gold and blue. Every time I put on the colors, I know I am representing y'all. For once, though, the spotlight is off me.

Maybe this all makes sense to you and you understand now. The last two seasons have been interesting!

I just have a few questions, since you asked me if I had any:

1. Why, all of a sudden, do you care if I'm not there?

2. Do you think it would make a difference if I were physically there?

3. Do you really want me there?

4. How do you even notice out of the sea of faces if I'm really there?

Cheers!

Me

The Prayer of Hope and Fate!

Dear God,

Someone once told me
When it comes to love
You have to make that giant leap
And take the risk of
Putting your heart on the line
I've been heartbroken
So many times
Because often
I believed that feelings I felt
Were those of "romanticism" and of "love"
However, my heart, eyes, and mind
Were simply deceived
For my feelings were not returned
As I secretly hoped

Furthermore,
I have come to believe
That I'm either incapable of
Knowing what love is or
Someone being able to feel for me as I for them
And share the compassion and romanticism

Although
A few have tried to convince me
That my little theory is
Mere hogwash
And that indeed
I am capable of being loved in returned
And in fact I do, too
Know what love is

That is why I ask
My Father in heaven
To give me the guidance and strength
To have my eyes, heart, and mind open
So that I may be able to see love
And that I may have the strength
To take that huge leap of fate
And for once
Know that by taking a risk
My heart shall not be broken

I ask all these things in your name

Amen

Dear Searching Soul Looking for Mine

Dear searching soul looking for mine,

I'm not sure where to begin or what to say to you if we ever meet, or have we already met and neither of us are certain? So I'll just start from the top as my heart speaks.

I'll never forget that cold and rainy January night we met. Sometimes, when I walk into our "place," all I can do is simply smile and think about this man who just came over, didn't know me from a hill of beans, and started talking to me. If you can remember, I was extremely furious and upset because I had just gotten into a fight with my best friend's girlfriend. Somehow, you merely listened to me vent, providing nothing but positive feedback.

During the spring, time seemed to slip away, and you and I became really good friends. It seemed every time you saw me, you'd always compliment or say something flattering. I believe the first time would have been on March 20, the Friday after spring break, the first time you'd really seen me outside the gym. Your words of compliments, I'll never forget them. "Dang, girl, look at you. You're looking really good." Why I remember those words I'm not sure, but I do remember we talked for about twenty minutes.

Time just seemed to slip away whenever we'd talk. I'll admit, I got scared around April, and all I wanted to do was my annoying venting, pushing you away. I guess you can say I don't like to get close to people if I know I'm going someplace. Especially men, because well, to be honest, all the men in my life have seemed to walk out.

Yet every time I did something, you'd always provide that moral support. Those sweet words. And always remember what I did and what I did not. Wow!

I haven't the slightest clue where you came from, but as time progressed, we seemed to connect and become friends, always losing track of time whenever we'd talk.

I'll never forget the day I told you I wasn't leaving and how your handsome eyes lit up. Then on that first full week of school when you saw me, you gave me a hug, out of the blue!

Nor will I forget on the day I was down and you sat beside me and started talking and all. It seemed since then, we'd make it a little ritual of randomly seeing each other and having lunch with each other.

I could go on in words, but I just know you're the most polite man I know. So full of manners, kindness, and thoughtfulness. A man who never forgets. A man a part of me only dreamed existed. Now here you are in my life; after trying to push you away, you stayed. All I know is that every time I'm with you, I can truly be myself, forgetting about what has happened in the past, where I have been, just living the moment. Being able to be a silly ol' blonde and a goober who talks a lot.

You've opened my eyes and showed me so many great things. I just know the worst part of this situation is that you're coming back into my life when everything's getting back on track, and I know what I want to do, and nine months from now, I won't be here, and you'll be off working.

I just know, if I get to know you any more and vice versa, I have this feeling the person I dreamed never existed is only staring me straight in the face.

Maybe you were right on that afternoon when you said that it felt more like a lifetime.

I just know, mystery soul, I don't want to fall for you, only to ruin the friendship and push you out of my life.

So you see, this is what I've been dying to tell you: I love how we can talk about sports, life, astronomy, and such.

I just hope that maybe one day, too, you'll find me and tell me how you're feeling.

I'm sorry for this letter being so long, but well, I must stop before I go on.

One day, I hope that you can read this letter and come find me.

Just always know my soul is yours always, my best friend.

Love,

The soul you've been looking for

Chapter 14

Simple Song and Dance

You always feel better when you sing. Music touches people's hearts. You know, it doesn't go through your mental capacity, it just moves you and it will let you cry.

—Jewel

I absolutely love singing. Music feeds my soul and touches my heart. As I have written each of these songs, I can only imagine others singing the lyrics and inspiring those around them.

Mr. Perfect

I've always dreamed of the perfect man
About six feet tall
Blond hair, boundless blue eyes
Athletic stature
Any girl's dream
A little bit of Southern comfort
A heart full of compassion and love
But mainly a godly man
Who can stand
This crazy dream

But sadly, that whole vision
Disappeared some time ago
When I met a man
Or should I say, a boy
Who met all my criteria
Had my heart
Made me feel on top of the world
Turned out to not be so perfect
Deep down in his heart and soul
He still needed work
For he was too far gone
And it only took me
The first twenty-four years of my life
To figure it all out
That perfect didn't exist
Yeah, perfect didn't exist
So I just threw that list away
And forgot about trying to wait for
Mr. Perfect

Now that I'm twenty-five
I feel free as a bird
Trying to just live
Not worry about Mr. Perfect
Thinkin' about him
How we'll have our happily ever after
Rootin' for each other
Being each other's best friend

I used to wonder
What it'd be like
To find a future coach or doctor
To sweep me off my feet
Spend our time
Discussing books, life, sports, music
And about our devotion to God
As we walk along the shores in the sunset
Mostly finding I'm falling more in love
With a man
Who loves God more than I do
But now it's a hazy vision
Truth is

Will, one day
The man God's planned
Be better than the one
I used to dream of?
We'll just have to
Wait and see
If throwing a list away
Was the best thing to do
Lord, please help me

So this crazy dreamer
Is going about her ways
Seeing the world
Touching lives

Making a difference
And seeing if
Maybe one day she'll
Have someone to share it all with
But for now
This is the way
Oh yeah, this is the way
It has to be

I Just Wanna Be Free

I've been traveling this unmarked road called life
Only to discover it's been
Full of the unexpected
You might as well just
Call it the blessed broken road
God's sure had his hand in it
He's sent me amazing angels
To watch over me and help me
I couldn't ask for more
No matter what happens
My faith's stronger than anything
Only time can tell
What'll happen and where I'll end up
Just know . . .

I wanna be free
I just wanna be me
I just wanna be who I am meant to be
For I know I am whole and complete
I am a child of God
Serving him and praising him
Trusting him with my life
Letting go of my past
Only living each day to the fullest
Loving with all my heart
And praying for all I meet
So Lord, just let me be and free me
Yeah, yeah, yeah . . .

Well, my heart's been broken, duct-taped, glued, and put back together
I know who I want to put all the blame on
But I'll tell ya
I have no shame

I may have believed
I found my perfect match
Yet once I discovered the truth
You might as well have lit that match
Because honey
Perfect wasn't everything
He didn't complete me
Because I am whole
And he brought me down sometimes
Most of all
I couldn't trust him
So now I sing out loud . . .

Now that it's all been said and done
I'm putting my trust in the hands of the Lord
Seeking him every moment and with every breath I take
Seeing who he's placed in my life
The people I can trust and count on (always)
Not having to worry or fear
This is the time to change for the good
A time to do what's right
Regain focus and get on the right track
Oh, oh, oh
Believing one day
I'll conquer the world
Seeing all things are possible
Being able to trust with all my heart
Keeping my faith going strong
Letting it all go, oh, oh, oh
Lord

I just wanna be

God's in Control and I'm Never Letting Go

It's amazing how life is
And many blessings we've all been given
I know sometimes I'm speechless and motionless
Unable to begin to explain it all
Just thanking God every day
None of this making any sense
Trying for the answers to figure it out
Solve the riddles
So where do I begin

Staring at you
Gazing into your eyes
As you stood there
That's a memory I'll forever hold on to
It's like you're embedded in my heart and soul
Still, I'm at peace with you
I know this sounds crazy
It's like either sinking or swimming
But I'm glad you're here with me
It's like the one I once knew
Had decided to appear again
But for how long will he stay
Will he stay
In my mind and in my heart
I know, Just pray
God'll give me the strength
To grasp onto this
Never letting go
Oh, never letting go

So I finally began to see
That none of this was a waste of time
Life's full of ups and downs

And reading between the lines
Still, I know God has his plan for me
Has a purpose for why people
Have been blessed into my life
Even if I try to fight it
God's strength is more powerful
And he knows what's best
Especially when I feel lost
Then I find myself
Thinking of someone
Who inspires me and moves me
So I stand there and sing

It may seem that I've been lost
But now I've found myself
In a state of grace and contentment
I know exactly where I am
I'm home
Oh, home, yeah
When I'm here
I feel like I could dance underneath the Texas stars
Run in that field of bluebonnets
Or let my hair down
It's like dancing in the rain
Washing my pain away
Wishing you could enjoy the ride
But all I can say is

Oh, I'm never letting go
For you've inspired my soul
And God's in control

What Do You Say to That?

This song is dedicated to the one with blue stained-glass windows!

There you sit
Pretty content with your life
Trying to just get by
Making it through the tests
Presented to you
And the ones ahead of you
Unsure of what's going on
But you sit back and ask
What she sees
When she looks at you

She says

As I gaze into your eyes
I see a set of stained-glass windows
Full of mystery
Just waiting to be solved
The more one admires the works of art
The more one becomes captivated
And lost in a sea of bright and boundless blues
Setting sail on a course
Only God knows where it's going
All in due time
He'll make it known
The answers one's been waiting for
Now what do you say to that?
Oh, what do you say to that?

As time surpasses them
All gathered in the bleak room
White as winter snow
Conversation carries on

A little of the unknown surfaces
You appear to become intrigued
Curious of what she's saying
You seemed to be inspired
And motivated to ask her
What she's thinking
But

Before you know it
It's all about reading between the lines
Trying to justify her way of thinking and feeling
Trying to understand her loving way with words
Hopefully understanding her logic
Holding onto her intentions
Still, you know she's observing you
Watching your every move
Seeing your reaction to her notions
But all you can do
Is ask her what she sees
When she looks into your eyes
As her compassion unfolds

She tells you
"Just know your eyes say
More than one can ever predict or know"
She knows when she looks at you
She sees right through you
Knowing you're a man of God
Full of love, kindness, and compassion
Something often forgotten and not realized
So true to that (yes, true)
You sit in disbelief
Yet all you can ask her is
How she sees all this

Now what do you say?
What do you say, bright eyes?
Oh, what do you say, bright eyes
To all of that?

Hiding from the Spotlight

Every single day
I walk down the road
Thanking God for all my blessings
Some I don't deserve, I believe
Yet I know God has His plan
And will provide me with all I need
Oh . . . oh . . . oh . . .
I couldn't ask for more
But there's just one thing
I wish I could burst out singing

Underneath my baby blues
Lies a mystery waiting to be unveiled
A mystery to a world
Full of love, life, Christ, and so much more
A heart full of purity and gold
All it takes is a little time
Out of your busy life
To sit down and engage in getting to know
The not-so-mysterious and complicated girl
I am acclaimed to be
Though I may not publicly show my ultimate feelings
Privately I'll let you know
Exactly what I'm truly thinking, feeling, and believing
I just want to hide it all away from the spotlight

People pass me by
I flash them a simple hi or hello
With a Southern smile
Showing my Texan hospitality
That I've been raised on
Never letting them see
I'm flying on the edge of my seat

Seeing where God's taking me
On my second chances
On this blessed road of redemption (yeah)
Because

It's hard to show the truth
Of what has held me back
When I'm ready to leave it all
In yesterday
Forgetting the pain
Of every heartache and devastation
The hurt and the scars
Finally overcoming all my fears
Putting myself back together
Being able to feel again
And know it's possible to let someone in
But only time can tell
So open up your eyes to see
I just need you to be patient and understanding
Willing to take that chance

I know I may come across
As one heck of a mess
Complicated and confusing at times
Please don't be scared
I'm not trying to intimidate anyone
Push anyone away
Or make someone go runnin'
It's just all of this is so new
Hopefully the world can understand that
I don't want to wear my heart on my sleeve
I just am ready for the changes
God has in store
Not trying to be in the spotlight (spotlight)
As I'm living out my dreams
Can you see

Hiding from the spotlight
Yeah . . .

I Know I'm Not Alone

I'm feeling alive
I'm feeling free
I just want to let my hair down
And run in the wind
I just want to shake it off
All the bad things that have happened to me
None of that matters now
Now that I see
Who I really am
Where I'm going
All because

I know I'm not alone anymore
I know I'm able to break my chains
I know that I'm saved by grace
Love's surrounding me every day
I am healed by His mercy
I am fortunate to have
Angels at my side
Guiding me along the way
Nothing can explain
What I'm feeling in my heart
I know I can make it

The power of life overcomes me
As I realize my newfound strength
No more running from my fears
Just accepting all my blessings
Embracing the light
So it can shine through me
Letting the world see

No more being overwhelmed
With the fashions of life
The worries of yesterday are gone
I'm flying so high
I'm believing in myself again
And I see my dreams
Nothing in this world can hold me back
No more (no, no)
So . . .

Yeah, I know I'm not alone
Yeah, I know!

You Don't Know What You Do to Me

You don't know what you do to me (yeah)
You don't know what you do to me
You don't know how you drive me crazy
How you push me to do my best
Inspire me in more than one way
Being around you
Helps brings out the best in me (oh, oh)

I just wish I could tell you
What my heart's secretly holding in
Maybe you'd be able to understand
How with you
I know God's placed you in my life
And I wouldn't change it
No, I wouldn't
Or have it any other way
Even though I may not show it
I'd wait patiently to see
If there's even a chance
For you to know
How I see you, believe in you
And can only pray
We only have the rest of our lives
To see where this journey is going to take us

All we have is time
God's time, you've said
And I'm learning that surely but slowly
It's something you've shown me for sure
You've opened my eyes to a new world
Over this short period of time
So I'm finding myself in a place
Conquering fear and allowing myself to feel

Trying not to overanalyze it all, yeah
It's something new
Something I've never known before
But . . .

When I felt like pushing and pulling from you
There was just something about those stained-glass eyes
I could see beyond the surface
I tried to ignore it at first
All I wanted to do was solve the riddle
But then things changed
I was stopped in my tracks
With you there was someone
I was the real me with
Forgetting the past and unashamed
And I could see the heart of a man
Touched by the light and saved by His grace

So I'm saying
You may drive me crazy
But I couldn't ask for more

I'm Alive and Fearless

Woke up this morning
To the sounds of a train rollin' into town
Looked at the clock
Quarter past five

I was up and couldn't go back to sleep
Jumped out of bed
Turned on the radio
Began to dance around
Thinkin' to myself

I feel so alive
I feel so free
I know He blesses me with the tiniest blessings
I know I can sing His song
I know I am thankful
I know I love Him
He's helping me to see
I'm fearless and I can fly
Sitting back, enjoying the flight

I roll out the door
And go do my normal routine
There's no sun in the sky
Just the stars and the moon
Shining bright to light my way
After an hour or so, feeling sexy and free
I come out to see
The sunshine rising on me
All I want to do is shout

Come back to see
What the rest of the day

Will have in store for me
It seems to be a typical day
I'm still flying free and fearless
Feeling on top of the world
Ready to face whatever challenges
Might happen to cross my path
I know in my heart
Because of my faith and trust in God
I'm not afraid
Oh, yeah

Who would've expected that
My day would see a twist
When a mysterious challenge
Entered through the door to my left
No one could have expected
The little show that was put on display
I was so caught off guard
But I know I wasn't afraid
All I know is
I can see past through
Those stained-glass blues
My confidence was sent soaring
But I knew I was on to something
Don't you know

Oh, I can't wait to see what
The rest of the day brings me
I just know I'm alive and fearless

A Little Prayer of Help

Here's a little song I wrote while watching a movie, which I had in my head for several days.

Papa, I wonder if you can hear
This prayer I'm praying to you
Right here, right now
I feel I need you more than ever
I don't want to walk
On that curvy unmarked road
Leading me straight to temptation's door
I just want to serve you
Answer your call
Use my gifts for your glory
And finish my education

Lord, here I am
Falling on my knees
Right at your feet
With my healing heart
And spirit-filled soul
I am yours and I am changing
I love you more every day
Yes, I'm afraid
But I'm walking by my faith
So can't you hear my plea
See, I need you now and forever
And know I am yours

Every day I walk the streets
People wave hello or flash a smile
I get a door held open for me
Someone stops me across the hall

Bittersweet conversations shared
This may sound crazy
But is this part of the plan or temptation
Oh, help me
So . . .

None of this makes sense to me
I know I am alive and blessed
It's all because of you
You've created me in your likeness and image
You've made me beautiful and strong
I am so ever thankful
Yet sometimes I'll admit
My emotions can make my mind play tricks on me
Yeah

Help me, Lord
Please help
Amen

Work in Progress

He'd never understand
How I hide behind
All the positives and my faith
He'd never believe
All the things I'm burying
Deep down in my heart and soul
I know he wouldn't believe
Any of it
He doesn't understand
Why I have to be this way
Although I want to tell him
Everything
And to make him see
Why with him I can be me

But what does it matter
I know he's going through a lot
I can see it in his eyes
And feel it in his touch
Only time and faith
Can heal
That broken heart of his
Lord, I hope he knows
I want to be there for him
Like any friend should
But I don't know how
For all I want is the truth
To be sung out loud
Like it should
Be sung

They say that
The truth can set you free

But is it really so
Especially when it's
Completely hard to believe
Yet you know deep down
It would make everything
So crystal clear
The eyes can only say
So much
To another soul

I hate complications
And right now
I see them happening
If the truth is revealed
Before he's ready to know all
Everything seems to be
Moving way too fast
So to avoid complicating
Anything in our friendship
It'll just have to be
My silent, unsung song
Lord, all I ask from you
Is to give me strength
Whatever path
You're sending me down

One day he'll know all
The demons I'm fighting
And understand why
I am the way I am
And all my struggles
I've been faced with
I've lied and been jealous
Lashed out when I've felt betrayed and angry
I've even done some things
I'm not proud of
Not to mention
Some things I'm burdened with

Not even my own best friend
Will ever know about
Sometimes the truth
Is too painful to bear

Sometimes our songs of truth
Have to wait
To make their debut
Until those broken hearts are healed
And God has blessed us with
That chance
To make it be heard
And their understanding
Is our song's blessing and encore

Then You Walked In

I don't know
How this all happened
Everything seemed to be
Going just according to plan
I was on a mission
To get my life in order
Beginning with
Getting rid of
All your guys and *you*
Forgetting about everything's that happened
Being free from all those basketballs and hoops
Then you walked into my life
And I got scared
The first moment we talked
I couldn't help but feel as if
I could fall for you
Taking the risk
Of letting my heart
Get broken again by another guy
To give someone a chance
To get to know me
And win my heart and trust again
Just to awake from this dream
And to realize
You are just one of them
A man who lives on the court
Married to his basketball
A type of man that I promised myself
I'd never again make the mistake of falling for

The next part of my plan
Is to continue training hard
Dedicating as much time as possible

To the sport that I love
My only escape from reality
Forgetting about basketball, your guys
And all those darn distractions
Including you
Just to complete my mission

Step 3 of my mission
Was to get my head on straight
Clear my mind
And regain my focus
On my education and music
Getting myself on the right track
To continue prepping myself
For Butler and saving the world

The last step in completing my mission
Was to build this barricade
Strong enough to withstand
Anything or any man, as a matter of fact
That would hurt me or
Keep me from achieving the first three parts
Of my mission and life plan
No matter what it took
Or what price I had to pay
Oh yeah

Now what am I going to do
Fail my mission
Or follow my heart?

Epilogue

So Surreal!

I had an *amazing* dream last night. So amazing I didn't want to wake up. I can't tell you when in the past twenty-five years I had a dream that was so real. I mean, I've had a bucket list of dreams I have wanted to achieve, but nothing like this before. Crazy part is, a part of me hasn't had this feeling since I was abroad almost eight months ago. (Really, I was in Sydney, the historic and beautiful Sydney, New South Wales, Australia!)

I can tell you I would never change a moment of those two months there. Each day, it felt like I was waking up in a dream or a fairy tale. After walking out of the room, I'd go to the balcony and see Moore Park and the golfers having tee time. Still, being home six months, I can close my eyes, imagine myself walking the subway of Central Station, exploring the mall in Bondi Junction, walking along the Sydney Harbour, or taking a ride on the ferry from the harbor to Manly Beach or Darling Harbour.

So here we are, almost six months since I have been back in Texas, and my heart feels completely torn. A part of me is completely lost, and I am only walking on faith and the grace of God. No matter how supportive my family and close friends have been, it has been a wreck of things.

My daddy has always told me, the more and more you lie about something, the lies just keep on building and they are going to eventually erupt. Lately, I feel I could be wearing a mask and hiding from the truth. The truth of how hard it's been for me to be back and the truth about why I fear seeing this coming weekend.

Almost a year ago, I wanted clarity, understanding in a friendship, and to figure out why I was not getting the blame for why our paths never crossed again. For two months, I really felt like I knew my friend and appreciated every moment spent. A part of me wondered if this person would be that friend who surprises you at the airport, but I was wrong. Now, all I want to do is scream and try to explain how I'm going one direction and that person's going another.

Let's jump now to the present day. It's hard to believe I've made it one year and have not allowed my heart to be fooled and fall in a deep crush for any male. Maybe I learned my lesson the hard way at this time last year. Who knows?

Now this dream has me feeling things I have never felt before, allowing my heart, soul, and mind to feel something that was so real. It's funny how you read about people getting angry at each other, ending up connecting, falling for each other, and then one has to move away. (Sigh . . .) It was, in its own way, perfect.

The dream seemed to be so perfect, just like in some odd way, my time in Sydney the first time and, now, the second time. I can only wish I could go back to find my heart. Life just seemed so surreal and on the right track. Spiritually, educationally, emotionally, physically, and athletically, everything seemed so harmless.

God, hello? Any response? All I can say is, God has a plan, and I guess eventually he has us wake up for a reason!

Fairy Tale: The Princess Went to the Ball

There once was a princess living in a world of modernity. On a very warm autumn day, she had been invited to attend the ball. For years she longed to be a part of the crowd, but a part of her only wanted to blend in. Still, days and weeks before her invitation, she would tell folks it would be a cold one before she did.

The day of the ball came, and her emotions were mixed. She knew her father had something planned, yet she wasn't certain.

Still, she got dressed in the appropriate colors, got all dolled up, and felt so natural.

Upon her arrival, people were very surprised she was there. However, she was able to blend in and enjoy the festivities, overall embracing the moments being presented.

When the ball ended, she found herself being dragged down to greet the knights by one of the youngest royals in the crowd. This took her by surprise.

Left without words, she followed the knight in training.

The next moment seemed still, like frozen sands in an hourglass. A silent film was being displayed. Only God's work was at hand.

When time had elapsed and the film had ended, the princess saw the little future knight run off, and she captured the moment. She left the grounds of the ball, remembering the day, thanking her father and smiling. Yet in her heart of hearts, she could only hold the truths.

She understood in life, it is all about timing. Not her time. Her father's time.

She experienced not the romanticism of a fairy tale but the beautiful blessing of it. One day, when the time is right, a knight will become her prince, who, like her, is imperfect and driven. Yet from the moment at the ball, she was able to grow up and see the blessings of knowing who you are and living for yourself.

Printed in the United States
By Bookmasters